The 12 DOGS of CHRISTMAS

By Steven Paul Leiva

Photographs by Ken Kragen

Based on the screenplay by Kieth Merrill

Story by Kieth Merrill and Steven Paul Leiva

Based on the book *The Twelve Dogs of Christmas* by Emma Kragen

And a screen treatment by Steven Paul Leiva

THOMAS NELSON
Since 1798

NASHVILLE DALLAS MEXICO CITY RIO DE JANEIRO BEIJING

Photographs by Ken Kragen; photograph of Emma on the train by Don Muirhead

Published in Nashville, Tennessee, by Thomas Nelson. Thomas Nelson is a trademark of Thomas Nelson, Inc.

Thomas Nelson, Inc., titles may be purchased in bulk for educational, business, fundraising, or sales promotional use. For information, please email SpecialMarkets@ThomasNelson.com.

Library of Congress Cataloging-in-Publication Data

Leiva, Steven Paul.

12 dogs of Christmas / by Steven Paul Leiva based on the screenplay by Kieth Merrill ; story by Kieth Merrill and Steven Paul Leiva based on the book The twelve dogs of Christmas by Emma Kragen.

p. cm.

ISBN-13: 978-1-4003-1053-1 (tradepaper)

ISBN-10: 1-4003-1053-9

I. Merrill, Kieth, 1940– II. Kragen, Emma. Twelve dogs of Christmas. III. 12 dogs of Christmas (Motion picture) IV. Title. V. Title: Twelve dogs of Christmas.

PZ7.L53724Aad 2007

[Fic]–dc22

2007013515

Printed in the United States of America

07 08 09 10 11 HCI 9 8 7 6 5 4 3 2 1

For my daughter Miranda
Dog lover *nonpareil*

Contents

Acknowledgments

The author wishes to give his thanks and admiration to Ken Kragen, gentleman and scholar of the sky. Appreciation must be given to Kieth Merrill and the full cast and crew of the film, *The 12 Dogs of Christmas*, for without them there would never have been this novel. I'm sure Ken and Kieth join the author in thanking Emma Kragen for her doggone wonderful and lyrical changes to an old classic, thereby making a new classic. And everyone involved in this project must give thanks to Amanda Martin for always holding things together with wit and charm, only two of the many attributes the author married her for.

Prologue

Max was a Poodle. Not one of those little Poodles, a Miniature or a Toy with puffy and fluffy fur finely cut and clipped like bushes in a French garden, who spent their days sitting in the laps of ladies who also seemed finely cut and clipped. No, Max was not one of those Poodles; Max was a Standard Poodle, proudly standing two feet tall, and although he was well groomed, it was not in a puffy and fluffy way but in a handsome boy-dog way with a coat of beautiful black curls.

Max had led a privileged life. He was the pet of Thaddeus Whiteside, the kindest man on the Upper East Side of New York City. Max's life had been one of warmth and food and love and play. Especially play, for Mr. Whiteside, despite his hair being as white as white could be, was more like a human boy who liked to laugh a lot than he was like the other men who used to come to Mr. Whiteside's beautiful four-story house on the Upper East Side to talk to him about what they called "business." Now Max did not know what business was, but it certainly was not play, because none of the men ever laughed about it.

"It's the Depression, Mr. Whiteside," one of the men had said one day. "You can no longer afford this house."

And then their beautiful house was not as warm, and the food was not as plentiful—but the love was just as strong, and Mr. Whiteside still laughed when they played . . . until the day when some other men came and started taking things away, including Max's big, beautiful doghouse that had always sat in a corner of Mr. Whiteside's bedroom and was Max's very special place.

Did all this make Max sad? Of course it did. And when a dog is sad, he can whimper to let his human know, but if a human is as kind as Mr. Whiteside, he doesn't have to hear his dog whimper, for he can see it in his dog's eyes.

Max's eyes never got so sad as when the other humans were moving things out, and Mr. Whiteside had to put Max in a wooden, cage-like box.

"I'm sorry, Max," Mr. Whiteside said. "I'm very, very sorry, but I can't take care of you any more. But you'll be okay, I promise. Look . . ." Mr. Whiteside picked up a copy of LIKE magazine, his favorite magazine because it always had big photographs he could show Max. "See this lady?" Mr. Whiteside asked, pointing to a picture of a woman in

front of a barn surrounded by a small group of dogs. "This is Cathy Stevens. They're calling her the Dog Lady of Doverville. Doverville is a town in Maine that has outlawed dogs! Can you imagine such a thing, Max, outlawing dogs? But since this Cathy Stevens actually lives just outside the town limits, she's set up a dog orphanage to take in all the dogs the townspeople have to give up. Well, I figured if she can take in Doverville's dogs, she can take in one more dog from New York City. So that's why I've put you in this traveling case and . . ."

Mr. Whiteside stopped talking when he heard a big crash coming from outside. He rushed to the window, opened it, and looked down one story to the street below where all his beautiful things were being loaded onto a truck.

"Please be careful with that dresser! It belonged to my mother!" Mr. Whiteside yelled down below.

And from below came a not-so-friendly voice that said, "What do you care? It's not yours anymore!"

And now, as Mr. Whiteside turned away from the window, Max saw the sadness in his eyes. It was a sadness he had never seen in Mr. Whiteside before . . . and a sadness he would never see in Mr. Whiteside again. At that moment, one of the other big men came and took Max away. They locked the box that looked like a cage with a shipping label that read: PLEASE DELIVER MAX TO THE DOG LADY, C/O DOG ORPHANAGE, DOVERVILLE, MAINE.

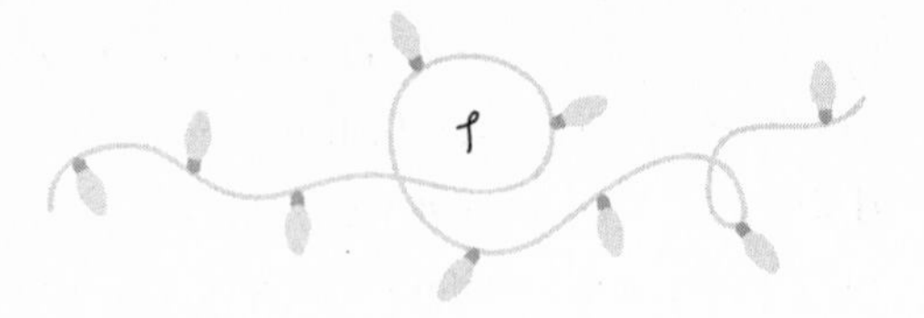

Emma

Emma O'Connor was a tomboy. Whether she was a natural tomboy or a tomboy because of her circumstances, even she was not sure. She might very well have liked to have worn pretty and frilly dresses, and she might very well have liked to have gone to fancy tea parties, but she lived in Pittsburg in 1931 when the country was suffering through the Great Depression, a time when very few had the money to be frilly or fancy. And it was just she and her father. Her mother had died several years before, and her father knew nothing about the raising of girls. So he dressed her in knickers—those funny boy pants that never made it down to the ankles—when she went to school, and he dressed her in an old pair of his overalls—slightly adjusted for her size—when she went to work.

Even though she was only twelve years old, it was necessary for her to work to help earn enough money for them to live. Her father worked every job he could find, but there just weren't that many jobs for men those days. So Emma delivered the *Pittsburg Herald* to all who could afford the luxury of a newspaper. Once a week she also collected all the bacon grease that her neighbors had saved for her in empty coffee cans. She could sell the grease for a few dollars to a company that used it to help make soap.

Emma O'Connor was a tough kid. Not mean, mind you, she was anything but mean, but tough—because she had to be.

It was the beginning of the Christmas season, and no twelve-year-old girl could be tough when visions of brightly wrapped presents appeared out of nowhere, and desires for a warm hearth and hot cocoa kept tugging at her, but had nowhere to take her.

Is it any wonder that Emma was a bit sad when she was finishing up her paper route that day? It was almost Christmas, and yet the headlines on her papers had nothing cheerful to report. And when she told Mr. Lawson that she was collecting for the paper that day, he said to her, with some embarrassment, "Can't afford it anymore, Em. Take us off your list." Then, as she did everyday, she walked past the local Hooverville, the empty lot where people who were homeless because of the Depression had built a bunch of makeshift shelters out of box-wood, cardboard, and scraps of metal. Well, that was sad every day, but even sadder around Christmas. Even the Salvation Army carolers, singing the songs Emma had always loved, seemed a little sad. Emma stopped to listen for a minute, gave them a smile, and wished she could have put a nickel into the collection pot, because poor as she was, she knew a lot more people had more reasons to be sad than she did. For at least she had her father, and he had her, and they had always taken care of each other, so everything—eventually—would be all right.

Wouldn't it?

When Emma got home to their dim, cold apartment, she found her father staring at an official-looking document. "Dad?" she said as she put down her paper route earnings on the desk. Her father, whose name was Douglas, looked at her and said straight out, because he knew his girl was tough, "Em, we've been evicted. We have to leave tomorrow."

"What?"

"We have to move out."

"Where are we going to live?" Emma asked, fearful of the answer. "Not the Hooverville, we aren't going to—"

"No! *We* are not. I'm going to send you to your Aunt Dolores."

"I have an Aunt Dolores?"

"I've never told you about her, have I? Well, yes, you do, sort of, it's a long . . . Look, she's a good woman, and I'm sure she'll take you in. She lives up in Maine, in a little town that I remember being quite beautiful called Doverville."

"But I want to stay with you!"

"Of course you do, honey. And I want you to, and you will again soon, I promise. But not right now. Right now I've got to figure out how to make things right, Em. I've got one last chance to be a very good father—and a very good man. I have decided that the country may be in a depression, but that doesn't mean *I* have to be. I'm not going to be. I'm going to go out there, no matter what the odds, and find a way to take care of you. But I've got to do it alone, Em. I can't ask you to go through what I may have to go through until I find that way."

Emma was confused. What her father was saying both comforted her—and scared her.

Emma did not sleep much that night. She passed the long hours weeping for her father and humming one of her mother's old songs. She alternated between the two, calming her sobs with the memory of her mother's song. She couldn't stand for her father to hear her cry through the paper-thin walls of her room. He had enough to worry about right now.

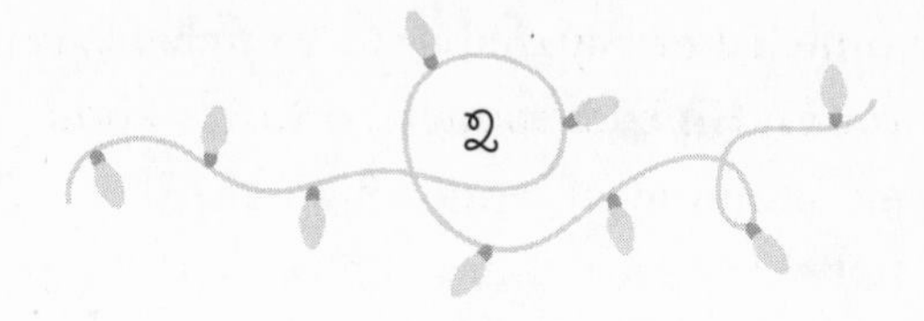

It's an Adventure!

The next morning Emma's father took her to Pittsburgh's Penn Station and put her on a train. Any other time riding the train would have been exciting. But all Emma and her dad could think about was that they were parting. Mr. O'Connor found Emma a seat, got her settled in, and ran his hands over the old wool cap he had given her to be sure it fit snugly on her head.

"Why do I have to go?" Emma asked for the hundredth time. "I want to stay with you!"

"I know, Em, but it's only for a little while. I'll come and get you before Christmas."

He had made this promise last night, hoping it would make Emma less sad. Christmas was less than a month away. But that's what worried Emma. How could her father find work *and* a new home in so short a time? A tear slipped down her cheek. But her father quickly wiped it away.

"Come on now; you're my tough girl."

Her father then took out of his pocket an envelope with a name, Dolores Snively, and an address written on it.

"You are going to like your Aunt Dolores. She can't wait to see you."

"You promise to come and get me?"

"By Christmas," her father reassured, putting the envelope in Emma's coat pocket.

"*Promise.*"

"I will," Douglas O'Connor said as emphatically as he could while holding back tears of his own. Then he hugged his daughter. Emma held on to her father tightly, but soon her father was gone, and Emma was alone.

A moment later, the train came alive and slowly lurched out of Penn Station, picking up speed and rumbling faster and faster away from Pittsburgh.

Emma just stared through the frosted window, into the gray, uncertain about the future she found herself traveling toward, about going up to this place called Doverville, Maine, and about going to live with an Aunt Dolores she hadn't even known existed. But most of all she worried about her father. What was going to happen to him? Was he going to have to live in a Hooverville, in some kind of a cardboard shack?

Because she had not slept the night before, the rhythmic sounds of the train soon helped worry give in to sleep.

Max watched in confusion as the humans carried him in his box that was like a cage down the stairs of Mr. Whiteside's house and out the back entrance and to a truck waiting in the alley. The men loaded Max onto the truck, and he braced himself as the truck rumbled and bounced through the streets of New York until it finally arrived at the freight loading dock at Grand Central Station. Then they loaded his cage into a train.

"Hey, George! Here's another one to Doverville. To that Dog Lady. Jeepers, this is becoming the Canine Express!"

Soon a huge door on the giant box was slammed shut, making everything dark. Max lay down with a whimper, wondering what was to come.

When Emma awoke, Pittsburgh was far behind her, and she was amazed to see a landscape of long stretches of farmland, dotted now and then with houses and barns. Emma had lived her whole life in Pittsburgh and had never been out of the city. She had never seen anything like this! She sat up straight to get a better view. *Hey,* she realized, *this doesn't look so bad. It could be an adventure!* Emma was always ready for a new adventure. Her dad would borrow pulp magazines from a friend and read her the adventures inside. He enthusiastically performed all the voices of the characters and became Emma's personal radio show. And in the library she had found and loved the adventures of Robin Hood and Tarzan and Little Orphan Annie. All those adventures had carried her out of the dreariness of the Depression, and out of Pittsburgh. But now here she was, on her own real adventure. She tried to think about the excitement that lay ahead, and not about her father left behind.

Eventually the train slowed as it came up to a huge city of unbelievably tall buildings.

"Excuse me," Emma said to a lady in fur who sat across the aisle. "Is that New York City?"

The lady in fur looked at Emma and smiled. "Of course it is, darling. The greatest city in the world!"

New York City! It was the city where she was going to have to change trains to catch the one going to Maine. *How will I . . . oh, all those people and all those trains!* Emma's thoughts raced until her hand came to rest on the envelope her father had given her. *It's an adventure,* she told herself. She remembered that the envelope held detailed instructions. *Like the clues to a mystery*, she mused. *I'll be okay. It's an adventure.*

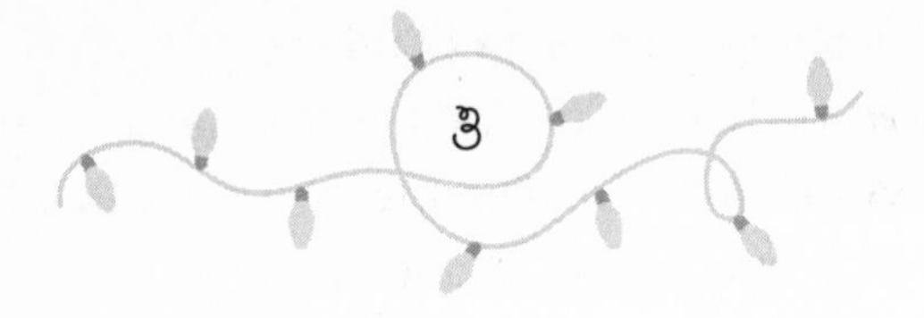

Doverville

Emma was amazed by Maine. It was snow-covered and beautiful, and everything was bright because the air was so clear, nothing like her Pittsburgh home. But it was still an unknown. She anxiously stepped off the train at Doverville Station. Emma took a deep breath, and like a good adventure hero, took the lay of the land.

The first thing Emma noticed were boxes and crates and carrying cases and cages being unloaded from the freight car of the train onto a large wheeled cart. And all of them contained dogs—all kinds of dogs, including two Dalmatians, a Golden Retriever, a couple of Beagles, a Chihuahua in a carrying case, and one large Poodle. There was also a woman all bundled up against the cold, and a young boy around

Emma's age similarly bundled, standing by a flatbed truck directing the freight handlers to load the dogs onto the truck carefully.

"They seem to be coming from all over, Mrs. Stevens," said one of the handlers.

"I know," said the woman. "It was the magazine article. I thought maybe the publicity would get me some donations. Instead it's just gotten me more dogs."

"Well, I suppose you don't have to take the delivery."

"How could I do that? Look at them. They're beautiful. And this Standard Poodle—what a handsome boy he is!"

A kind-looking lady looked through the slats of Max's cage and smiled at him, which was nice. But she was not Mr. Whiteside, and Max wanted Mr. Whiteside. "What's your name, boy? Oh, I see." The lady looked at the label on the cage. "It's Max. Well, Mike," she said to a boy standing nearby, "this is Max. We better get him loaded."

The boy came over and tugged at Max's cage, which was still on the freight cart, but the cage went nowhere. It seemed to be stuck on something. He tugged again, and again, and once more, which was not fun for Max, as it jerked him around in the cage. He wished the boy would stop. Then a girl walked up and said, "Here, let me help."

Mike, in the middle of his struggle with the Poodle's wooden cage, looked up to see where the voice had come from and saw who he at first thought was a boy. But the voice he had heard was a girl's, and the hair was long, blond, and in braids, even if it was covered by a man's cloth cap—much like the one Mike himself was wearing. Why Mike took an immediate dislike to Emma is a mystery. He glared at her as he jumped onto the freight cart to try to move the cage from a different angle, telling her, "I don't need help from a girl."

"Obviously you do," Emma observed, not understanding Mike's logic and jumping in to help by tugging on the cage as Mike tried to push it forward.

"No, stop," Mike insisted, alarmed at Emma's interference. "Stop!"

But Emma wanted to help and saw no reason why she shouldn't.

"Just leave it. Leave it!" he ordered.

Emma was not used to taking orders from boys—unless you count her father, which she didn't. So she tugged even harder at Max's cage.

Why were these kids pulling and pushing his cage so much? Max could hardly keep his footing, and he was scared, and so he growled at the kids. He had never, ever growled at kids before. Mr. Whiteside had not liked it.

"*I've* got it!" Mike tried to convince Emma as she made one last, big tug on Max's cage. Unfortunately she was tugging on the end that opened—and it did, releasing Max.

Freedom! Max bolted as fast as he could, away from the kids and away from the cage. And maybe, just maybe, he could find Mr. Whiteside.

"Aarrugh!" Mike yelled as he jumped down from the cart, landing with his face right in Emma's. "Girls are worthless!" he shouted at her, and then he took off, running after Max.

CHAPTER 3

Emma may have been tough—but not so tough that what Mike had said to her did not hurt. Girls were worthless? No, that's not what he meant; he meant that *she* was worthless. But she had only been trying to help.

None of this was funny, of course, but there was someone viewing it through a pair of binoculars that thought it was. His name was Melvin, and you should know right now that he is not going to be one of the heroes of this story. In fact, if any man in the town looked like one of the villains in the adventures Emma loved, it was Melvin. First of all there were the goggles he always wore, which gave a very insect-like look to his face, a look aided by the old leather aviator's cap pulled tightly down on his head, his gray and dirty beard, and his twisted smile that showed off his rotten teeth. Second of all were the old, worn, black leather jacket and the black shirt and the black boots he wore. We are very fortunate that Melvin rarely talked, for his voice most certainly could not have been pleasant. But why did he find the scene he had just witnessed funny? Possibly because he always found a chuckle or two in the misfortune of others, and most certainly because he knew his boss, Norman Doyle, would also find it amusing. Melvin couldn't wait to tell Norman, so he jumped on his motorcycle, roared the engine once, twice, and a third time, and then sped away to do that very thing.

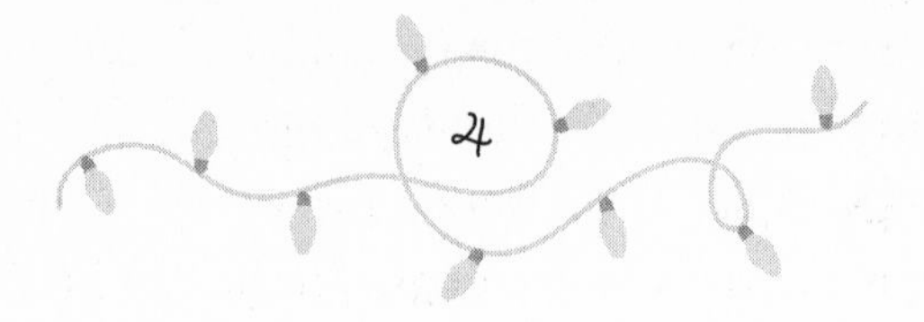

4

The Brothers Doyle

If Norman Doyle had had his way, Doverville would have been renamed Doylerville. His grandfather had been one of the founders of the town. His brother, Nobel Doyle, was the newly elected mayor of the town. And he, Norman Doyle, was about to be installed in the very important position of Town Dogcatcher, which was quite a promotion from his previous job as Town Garbage Collector. Now in most towns the position of dogcatcher, while not unimportant, was usually not considered *very* important. But this was Doverville, where dogs were outlawed, and in a town where dogs were outlawed, the Town Dogcatcher was as important as the Town Sheriff. It was actually more important, if you thought about it, which Norman did, despite how difficult thinking was for him, for the sheriff only had to catch human criminals, of which there were next to none in Doverville, it being a small, quiet town of fairly nice people. But the *dogcatcher* had to catch all the dogs. And there were now quite a few. And Norman loved catching dogs, for he hated dogs—hate, hate, hated them!

Why did Norman hate dogs? Well, maybe because some people just do. Some people just aren't dog people; some people are, like Norman, cat people, the best kind of people to be in his estimation. Or maybe it was because when Norman was nine and three quarters years old, he slipped and fell into a large pile of dog poop. This is bad in and of itself, but far worse when all the other kids see you do it and laugh at you in all the variations of laughter. Some of the kids chuckled, some guffawed, some tee-heed, some slapped their knees while howling, and some even snorted. And every one of these various laughs cut like a knife deep into Norman. He cried, he hid his face, and he never forgot it. And he might still be sitting in that dog poop if his big brother, Nobel, had not rescued him and driven the other kids away.

How times had changed. Now here they were in the town hall. Nobel, the mayor, was addressing the newly elected Town Council—all cat people good and true—who had all run on the same platform Nobel had run on. And nearby stood Norman, whom everybody had gathered in the town hall to see installed in the very important position of Town Dogcatcher.

Twenty-five years ago, the year of the great rabies scare, the townspeople passed City Ordinance 109, section 2, approved on December 19, 1906, that read in part: "Forthwith it shall be unlawful for dogs to reside, bark, breed, or foul the foot-ways within the city limits of Doverville." No one had enforced the no-dog law since 1907, the year the great rabies scare had ended. In fact no one had even remembered there still was such a law on the books—that is until Nobel discovered the law while looking for a campaign platform. He quickly took a poll and determined that there were more cat people in Doverville than dog people, revealing the preference of the majority, whose votes he wanted. And he knew his opposition would be weak, for there was a Depression going on, and a dog was just another mouth to feed. Nobel surmised that people might even like the excuse to get rid of the mangy mutts. Now that might have been so, and it might not, but what was definitely so was that Nobel ran unopposed, so he couldn't help but win. Nonetheless, he acted like he had won a major victory against great odds, strutting around in his three-piece suit and top hat, with a medal on his lapel that he considered to be his badge of office, but was really just a third-place medal he had won for a spelling bee in the fourth grade.

"The dogs will go!" Nobel declared to the town council and other cat-people citizens of the town. "That's what I promised—that's what I'm delivering."

The council and citizens gave him a rousing round of applause—including Norman, even while holding his beloved cat, Scratch.

"To help me in this momentous task, my friends, I have duly appointed Mr. Norman Doyle dogcatcher of Doverville!"

This was Norman's cue to immediately come up front and receive his share of applause. Soon Norman was up and standing beside his brother, smiling and nodding at the recognition, and hugging Scratch.

"Thank you, Nobel," he said. Then he became very solemn as he raised his right hand as high as one could while hugging a cat, and said: "On my honor I will do my best to do my duty to Doverville to keep dogs out of Doverville. Old Scratch here can smell a dog a mile away. And as for me, well, as you know, I hate dogs, I hate, hate, hate 'em."

The audience again erupted in applause as Norman hugged old Scratch and grinned.

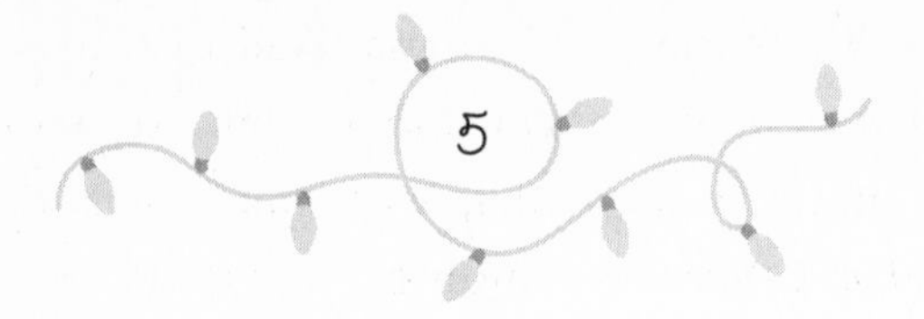

Aunt Dolores

Emma left the train station and started walking to her Aunt Dolores's house, following the directions her father had written down and put in the envelope along with the instructions of how to change trains at Grand Central Station. There was also a short note for Dolores that read: "Dear Dolores, Here's Emma as I wrote to you. Please make sure she goes to school. Thanking you in advance, Douglas O'Connor."

Doverville was a small, pretty town of white clapboard houses and red brick buildings. Maybe it was especially charming now that it was covered with snow and decorated for Christmas, but Emma thought that even in the summer, the town would be beautiful. The Christmas decorations did seem a little meager, but that was probably, like so many things, due to the

Depression. Still, there was the attempt to reflect the spirit of the season, and Emma liked that. And with the snow on the ground and the air so crisp and clean, Emma couldn't help but stop now and then and feel as if she were standing in the middle of a picture postcard.

Max ran and ran, but had no idea where to go, because wherever this was it certainly was not New York City, for all the buildings here were very small. And if it was not New York City, how could he ever find Mr. Whiteside? This place did, however, look a little bit like Central Park, where Mr. Whiteside always took Max for walking and running and playing with the ball. It had a lot of trees, and it was covered with the white cold stuff just like Central Park.

Max was tired and wanted to stop, but that boy was chasing him, and probably wanted to put him back in the wooden cage. Then the boy shouted out, "Max!" That's what Mr. Whiteside always called him. Maybe he knew Mr. Whiteside; maybe the boy would take Max to him.

Max dashed across a road, but stopped on the other side, turned around, and sat. The boy stopped. He was breathing hard. Max had noticed that before—humans don't run as well as dogs.

CHAPTER 5

"Here, boy," the boy said as he slowly approached Max. "Come here, Max. It's okay."

Max wasn't so sure about that, but he couldn't run forever. He let the boy come up to him and put a leash around his neck.

All of a sudden, there was the most awful sound. Max looked up to see a monster coming down the road.

Oh, no! Mike thought. *It's Mr. Doyle in that awful dog-catching machine of his.*

Coming down the road, heading straight toward Mike and Max was Norman Doyle and bug-face Melvin on a fearsome machine. It was basically an old motorcycle that Melvin had welded armor plating onto. He had also attached to it the most elaborate sidecar that wrapped around the back of the motorcycle. Bug-face Melvin was driving the Fearsome Machine, and Norman Doyle, the newly instated Town Dogcatcher, sat in the sidecar's strangely elevated seat. In back were a little truck-like flatbed on which was secured a cage for criminal dogs and a little case wherein old Scratch rode. Various dog-catching nets on the end of long poles flapped in the wind like pirate flags. Norman grabbed one to use on Max.

"Come on, Max, come on!" Mike yelled as he tried to pull the dog along. But Max was scared and didn't want to move. Norman was grinning in anticipation of his first official capture of a criminal dog, as they got closer and closer.

Norman's dog net was just swooping down when Mike's mother pulled up in her truck and slammed on the breaks, stopping right before Mike and Max, and blocking the path of the Fearsome Machine.

Cathy Stevens opened the passenger door of the truck and yelled to her son, "Mike, get in!" Mike lifted Max into the cab of the truck, then followed, slamming the door behind him. Cathy hit the gas just as Norman was running up to them.

"What are you doing?! Give me that dog!" Norman yelled as the truck sped away. He ran back to the Fearsome Machine and jumped on, ordering bug-face Melvin to "Catch that truck!"

Cathy Stevens drove as fast as she could, ever mindful of the snow-covered roads and the many dogs she had in the back. But she had to save them, for she had no idea what would happen to them if Norman Doyle got his dirty hands on them. She had known Norman since they were children, and she had never liked him. His personality was nothing to speak of, so she never did.

CHAPTER 5

"Faster, Mom, faster! Hurry!" Mike shouted. He had been watching the Fearsome Machine's progress and was alarmed that it was getting closer. But then they came to the old South Creek bridge, and in passing over it they passed a sign that read: LEAVING DOVERVILLE CITY LIMITS.

"He-he-he! Good-bye, dogcatcher," Cathy said as they headed off toward home.

Bug-face Melvin stopped the Fearsome Machine just before the bridge, and Norman jumped down from his high seat and looked after the truck full of dogs with great disgust. And then he went over to the case containing his beloved cat. "Don't worry, Scratch, we'll get 'em next time."

Douglas O'Connor's directions had been very clear, and Emma had no problems finding her Aunt Dolores's house. It was a white clapboard two-story house, with an old Model T Ford sitting in the front drive. There was a big oval sign in the yard nailed to two tall two-by-fours that read: DOLORES'S BEAUTY SALON. The oval was fringed with Christmas lights. When Emma got up to the front door, there was another sign that welcomed visitors to just walk on in, so Emma did, entering a small room that was wonderfully warm. She saw no one, but heard voices coming from a room to her left. Emma walked in.

The room, which had originally been the living room, had been outfitted with all the modern equipment of a beauty salon, including special chairs, two big dome hair dryers, a special sink to wash hair in, and several vanity tables with mirrors. Sitting at one of the vanity tables was a very large woman with the jolliest face Emma had ever seen. She could have been a young Mrs. Santa Claus. Standing behind the large lady, styling her hair, was a thin, middle-aged woman in a red dress. She might once have been very pretty, and was now still attractive, but had the kind of face that made it clear that she took nothing for granted and everything with a grain of salt.

"I'm Emma," Emma said quietly. "Are you Aunt Dolores?"

Dolores looked at the child before her, a girl, she guessed, not looking for a new hairdo, but certainly in need of one.

"Whatever you're peddling, I am not interested. Now get on out of here." Dolores waved her away with the comb she was using on the lady.

"My dad wrote to you that I was coming."

"Well, who's your dad?" Dolores asked, unimpressed.

Emma showed her the envelope. Dolores took it from her, seeing her name on the outside. She opened it, and the note inside flooded her with old memories, not all of them pleasant.

"You're Douglas O'Connor's girl?"

Emma nodded.

"That rat! I am *not* your aunt, and I am not the dummy he takes me for. Did he send you here?"

"He wrote you a letter."

"Well, I never got it. And you can just go right back and tell your dear daddy that your *Aunt* Dolores is dead and buried as far as he is concerned!"

Emma, of course, was now confused and scared, and anyone could see this if they were looking, which Dolores wasn't. Luckily, though, the jolly lady, whose name was Mabel, was.

"Where you from, sweetheart?" Mabel asked.

"*Pitts-burgh!*" Dolores answered for Emma. "The grave of the world."

"Well, you can't expect a child to find her way back to Pittsburgh."

"My dad's coming by Christmas," Emma said, hoping that helped.

And it may have, for Dolores stopped to think for a

moment, and the thinking seemed to soften her a little. "He's coming here?" Emma nodded, and there seemed a little more softening to be seen in Dolores's eyes—but only for a very brief moment. "Well," she said testily, waving Emma away, "go wait for him some place else."

To be told that she was worthless and then to be dismissed as a nuisance, all in one day, is not something that would make any child feel good, and Emma, at this moment certainly didn't. She slowly turned to go.

"Dolores!" Mabel admonished as she got out of her chair and walked toward Emma, holding out a hand. "For goodness' sake, you come back here, child." Mabel retrieved—and rescued—Emma just as she was leaving the room, then turned to glare at Dolores, her friend of many years, whom she knew for a fact was not as hard-hearted as she was pretending to be. Dolores looked at Emma, whose eyes were sad, and then back to Mabel, whose eyes were pleading. She lightly tapped her foot, thinking she would not budge, but found herself saying instead, "Okay," which delighted Mabel. "But look," Dolores now addressed Emma, "you need to get something real straight: I am not your aunt, and I did not get a letter. Your good-for-nothing father and I may . . . have . . . been . . . well, never mind. But don't you think for one minute you and I are family."

"You know," Mabel said to Emma with a jolly smile, "I'll bet you're hungry."

And she was. So Dolores fed her, telling her she was going to account for everything she cost, which Mabel thought was outrageous, and telling her she expected her to get a job, which Mabel thought was even more outrageous. But Dolores was determined, and Emma didn't mind, as she was used to working.

That night, lying in bed in Dolores's spare bedroom, Emma forced herself not to cry. *Adventure heroes don't cry*, she thought, *and this is certainly becoming an adventure.*

Max was glad that the boy had held him so tightly as they sped and bumped and turned sharp curves in the truck. It helped him to be less scared. When the truck finally stopped and the boy let him out, Max was hoping he was going to find Mr. Whiteside, but he could see him nowhere. There was a big building that the woman and the boy took Max and the other dogs to. Inside were several rows of pens where dogs were sleeping or eating or just scratching themselves. The woman and the boy started moving the new dogs to various pens, talking

to them in sweet voices that made all the dogs feel good. But Max did not want to go to one of the pens. He had never shared a space with another dog before. The boy tried to pull him on his leash to one of the pens, but Max stood his ground. Then Max saw in a corner of the big building a big wooden doghouse, almost like the one he had had at Mr. Whiteside's. Now he pulled the boy, trying to get to the doghouse.

"Let him go," the woman said.

"But, Mom, that's Yeti's."

"And Yeti hasn't used it since the other dogs arrived. So if Max wants to go there, let him."

Mike took Max off the leash, and Max dashed to the doghouse. Inside he looked and sniffed and turned around several times. It was not as large as his old doghouse, but he liked it still, and he decided that he would just stay in this doghouse until Mr. Whiteside came and got him!

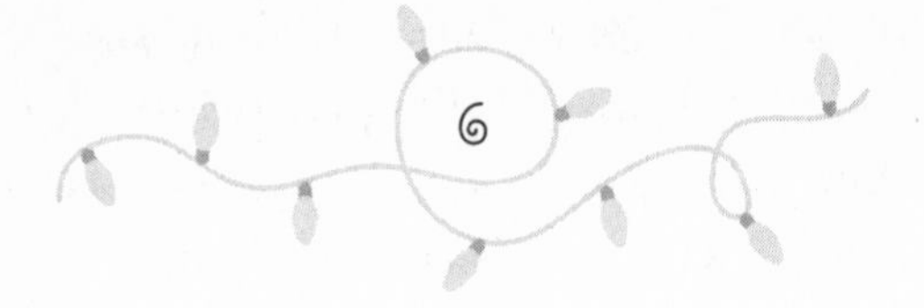

A Double Rescue

The next morning Dolores gave Emma directions to the schoolhouse, and a note for the principal, Mrs. Walsh, explaining that Emma was a visitor from out of town, and rather than have her sit around and be idle, she might as well be put in school.

As she was walking to school, Emma came upon two beautiful Cocker Spaniels. One was an adult with a black and white coat, and the other, although brown and white, Emma guessed was her pup. Emma had just stopped to admire them when suddenly an unkempt man with long, unwashed hair swooped down on the mother like a banshee from the Irish stories her father told her and captured the larger dog in a net. Then he picked up the dog and took her away. Fearing the Banshee Man would come back for the pup, Emma grabbed it and looked for a place to hide. Luckily there was an open shed nearby, and Emma ran into it, closing the door behind her. *Safe,* Emma thought, as she breathed hard, trying to shush the puppy who wanted to bark—and so did. Suddenly, the doors flew open, and the Banshee Man stood there silhouetted by the sun, a frightening figure. But that did not stop Emma from running hard into him, pushing him aside, and running fast with the puppy in her arms to escape.

The Banshee Man was, of course, Norman Doyle, and he was not happy to have been thwarted. He gestured off to the distance, and that gesture brought forth bug-face Melvin on the Fearsome Machine; Norman jumped on board and ordered Melvin to give chase. Emma had looked back and seen all this and, with the puppy snug in her coat, ran even harder down the road and into some woods until she found a tree to hide behind. But she could hear the Fearsome Machine come close and stop, and then she could hear the *CRUNCH-CRUNCH-CRUNCH* of the Banshee Man walking in the snowy woods looking for her. When the crunches got very close, Emma bolted and ran, constantly looking behind her to see how close the Banshee Man might be getting.

"Oomph!" Emma ran right into a big, bundled-up

old man in a fur cap with cold eyes and a gray beard. Was he another Banshee Man? The old man grabbed Emma and spirited her away!

Norman, who thought he knew which way the pesky girl had gone, now realized he had no idea where she was. He looked in front of him, and to the right. He looked to the left, and behind him. But nowhere could he see the girl. Suddenly he heard the infernal howling of hounds. He twisted around and flashing before him was a dogsled being pulled by seven powerful Huskies. On the runner sticking out behind the sled stood the big man with the gray beard. And in the bed of the sled lay Emma, holding the puppy tight and close, covered in a nice, warm blanket.

"Arragh!" Norman yelled, and he jumped back up onto the Fearsome Machine.

The chase was on! The old man with the gray beard mushed his dogs on faster and faster, and Norman bashed bug-face Melvin on the head to get him to catch up. Soon the Fearsome Machine was running parallel with the sled.

Norman reached and tried to grab the puppy from Emma's embrace. "Closer, closer!" he yelled at Melvin.

"Watch out!" Emma cried, watching the two contraptions almost collide.

Norman's glove-covered hand was just about to latch

on to the pup when the sled suddenly veered to the left at a fork in the road, leaving the Fearsome Machine to veer right and go off farther and farther away.

Emma looked up at her rescuer and smiled. The old man did not smile back. Soon he pulled up in front of Doverville School and stopped. "You should be in school!" the old man snipped, speaking to Emma for the first time. Emma got off the sled, and the old man was gone before she could thank him.

After an adventure like that, it seemed sort of anticlimactic to have to go to school. And what was she going to do with the puppy? She figured this Mrs. Walsh, the principal, could help, so she took the puppy along with her into the school.

She was wrong. Mrs. Walsh, with a face as sour as a summer lemon, told Emma, "It's an old wives' tale that dogs are good for girls. Get rid of that puppy immediately! And get back here fast so that you're not late for class!" Emma ran out of the school. She supposed she could have just let the dog go, but she knew its mother was gone, and the Banshee Man might come back, so she couldn't really do that. Outside, walking around the school, trying to figure out what to do, Emma saw a large storage shack attached to the back of the school. She looked in, and there was a perfectly good box that might be comfortable for the pup. She put him in, covered it with a plank of wood, and put a heavy brick on top. "I'm sorry I don't have food for you," Emma told the pup, "but I'll come back. I promise." The puppy whimpered in response as Emma ran back to the school.

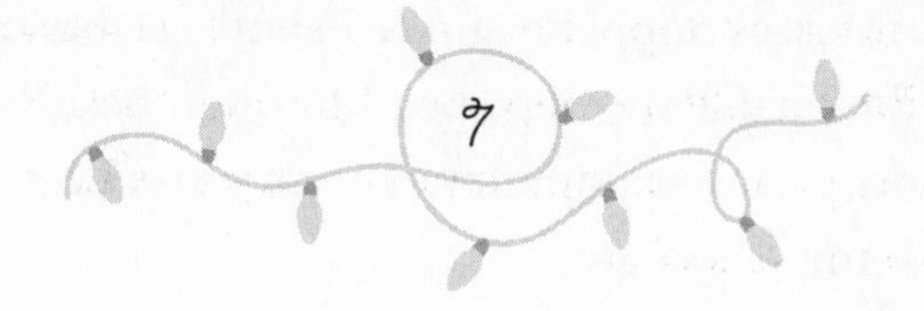

Puppy Love

Music greeted Emma as Mrs. Walsh escorted her into the school assembly hall. The class she was to join was rehearsing "The Twelve Days of Christmas" for an upcoming school program. The students, including Mike, were standing around a piano singing. "Eleven pipers piping," the voices rang out over the piano, played by their teacher, Mrs. Clancy, a pretty young woman whom Emma could see was very pregnant.

"Class," Mrs. Walsh said, "I would like you to meet Emma O'Connor."

The class looked at this new student very curiously, for they had rarely seen a girl in boy's clothes before.

"And where are you from, Emma O'Connor?" Mrs. Walsh asked.

CHAPTER 7

"Pitts—" Emma started to say. But after the last couple of days of upsets and rejections, Emma really wanted to make a good impression. And besides, was there ever an adventure hero from Pittsburgh? "I live in New York—the greatest city in the world."

"Well," Mrs. Clancy said, getting up from the piano bench with some difficulty, "welcome to Doverville, Emma. This is just perfect, because we've been looking, looking, looking for a partridge in a pear tree."

"I don't sing," Emma told her truthfully. "Anyway, I won't be here that long. My dad—my dad and *my mom* are coming to get me before Christmas."

Mrs. Walsh was shocked by Emma's brassy tone, but her attention was averted by the burst of a whole range of notes on the piano when Mrs. Clancy flumped down on the keys overcome by the sudden onset of labor!

Mrs. Clancy started breathing hard, and two of the girls, who had been rehearsed in more than just "The Twelve Days of Christmas," ran up to her and, each taking an arm, walked her out of the assembly hall. Mrs. Walsh, who really didn't like little matters like childbirth to upset her school day, had no choice but to cancel the rehearsal and, indeed, class for the rest of the day—which made not one student unhappy.

Emma had wanted to run out right away to check on the puppy, but Mrs. Walsh kept her behind to answer a few question about her previous school and other "facts" about her life. By the time Emma got out to the shed, she found the box empty!

"Is this who you're looking for?" came a voice from behind her. It was the boy from yesterday who had called her useless. "Look, you cannot keep a puppy in a dark box," Mike lectured. "He was crying. I could hear him from all the way in the front."

"Well, they took his mother!" Emma said, trying to explain her actions.

"The new dogcatcher?" Mike asked. Emma shrugged her shoulders, for she really didn't know. She took the puppy into her arms, and Mike could see that she was truly concerned about it. Maybe she wasn't so useless after all. "Look, do you want to take him to my house? We'll get him something to eat. We have lots of dogs."

When they got to the Stevens farm, despite the snow on the ground and the chill in the air, Emma felt nothing but warmth. Maybe it was because Mike was now being nice to her and was, Emma had to admit, kind of cute with his red hair and freckled face. Or maybe it was because Mrs. Stevens seemed genuinely happy to see her and welcomed her to their home. Or possibly it was because she found on the farm many happy dogs.

There were Dalmatians and Sheepdogs, and Boxers and Bassett Hounds. There were big dogs like St. Bernards, and little ones like Chihuahuas. There were Cocker Spaniels like the puppy, some Golden Retrievers, and even a Poodle in a doghouse. But the Poodle was different—the Poodle did not seem happy.

"This is Max," the boy said to the girl. It was the girl who had jostled his cage. Max was a little scared of her, but she was holding a puppy and loving it, so she must be okay. "Hey, Max!" said the boy as he started to rub him behind the ears. Max closed his eyes and nuzzled the boy's arm. "You going to come out, boy?" Despite the persuasive behind-the-ear rubs, Max still didn't want to come out. Not until Mr. Whiteside came to get him.

"He just won't come out," Mike said to Emma, while showing her the barn where the dogs slept.

"How come?"

"I think it's because he's so sad. He eats a little, not as much as he should. I wish we knew what was wrong."

Mrs. Stevens prepared a wonderful lunch, and as they sat and ate it, Mike explained how his mom had become the Dog Lady of Doverville and showed Emma the *LIKE* magazine. Emma was impressed; she had never had lunch with someone famous before. "Too famous," Mrs. Stevens said. "Now I have all these dogs coming from all over the country, and I don't know how I'm going to continue to feed them all."

After lunch, Mrs. Stevens called around to see if the puppy and her mother had belonged to anyone, but no one claimed the dogs.

"So what're you going to call him?" Mike asked, figuring the dog now belonged to Emma.

"I don't know," Emma said.

"Well, he's got to have a name."

She supposed he did, so she picked the name she liked the best. "Douglas O'Connor."

"You can't name a dog Douglas O'Connor."

"Why not?"

"Because it's just not a dog's name."

"Yeah, well, what about Yeti?"

Yeti was Mike's dog, a beautiful Sheepdog he had had since it was a puppy. There were a lot of wonderful dogs on the farm now, but Yeti was Mike's number one favorite. "Yeti is a perfect dog's name. My mom says it's '*fraught* with meaning.' See, look at her fur. It's like snow. Look at her face."

But you couldn't really see Yeti's face, and Emma said so. "Of course," Mike said, "that's why her name's Yeti. It's the name of the Abominable Snowman. Douglas O'Connor is the dumbest name I've ever heard."

Emma had not explained that it was her father's name, and she didn't want to now. "Well, he's not my dog anyway."

Mrs. Stevens offered to take care of the dog, and Emma agreed that was best. But as they started walking to the truck for Mrs. Stevens to drive Emma back to Dolores's, the puppy broke from his pen and ran into Emma's arms. "Well, it looks like you've got someone to look after," Mrs. Stevens said as she, Emma, and the puppy got into the truck.

On the way Mrs. Stevens cautioned Emma to keep the puppy hidden and told Emma that she would pick her up in the morning for school. "Sneak the puppy out, and I'll take it during the day," she said with a smile. "Got to keep it away from old Norman Doyle!"

When she got back to Dolores's, Emma wrapped the puppy in her coat and ran upstairs before Dolores could come out of the salon. As soon as she was in her room, she heard footsteps coming up the stairs. Hurriedly, Emma sat the puppy on her bed and threw blankets over him. "You get a job?" Dolores yelled out. "No," Emma yelled back, thinking that would stop her, but Dolores was unstoppable. "You better be getting a job and paying your fair share, or you'll be living in the woods. You hear me?" The door swung open, and there stood Dolores, one hand on her hip. "I'll tell you what. I know a fellow who will give you a job if I ask him. He practically worships the ground I walk on. Poor soul."

Emma, trying to still the wriggling lump on her bed, attempted to act normal and make conversation. "What does your boyfriend do?"

"He is *not* my boyfriend! He just thinks he is some hotshot 'cause he was promoted from garbage to animal control."

"You're going to get me a job with the dogcatcher?!"

Dolores nodded. "Just until your dad shows up—if he ever does." Then she left the room. Emma breathed a sigh of relief, and the puppy whimpered. Emma was just about to let him out from under the blankets when Dolores suddenly popped back in. "Look, you're whimpering like some little lost pup, and I'm only trying to help you."

"You don't need to bother the dogcatcher. I'll find a job. I promise," Emma said. But Dolores's attention had already moved to the braids coming out from under Emma's cloth cap. "Is that how you always wear your hair?" she said, taking some professional interest.

Emma just shrugged, wanting to engage Dolores as little as possible. And it worked—Dolores left. Emma rescued the puppy from the blankets, and the two snuggled up together on the bed. Soon they were both asleep.

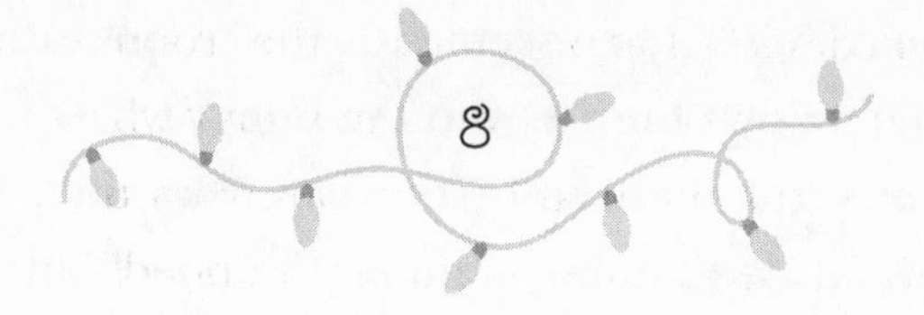

8

Old Jake

Mrs. Clancy brought into the world a beautiful baby boy, seven pounds, eight ounces. But that did not impress Mrs. Walsh, whose only concern was that now Mrs. Clancy could not bring into the world the Christmas program. She had to find someone else. She asked Mrs. Jones, the history teacher, but Mrs. Jones said she couldn't do it because she didn't have any music experience in her past. Then she asked Mr. Shaw, the biology teacher, but he said if he couldn't dissect it, he couldn't understand it. Finally she asked Mr. Cullimore, the school coach, who said sure—he was game for anything!

So Mrs. Walsh gathered all the students into the assembly hall and made the grand announcement that Coach Cullimore would now direct the Christmas program and the singing of "The Twelve Days of Christmas." She also seemed to take pleasure in announcing that Emma, who *would* participate in the program, was *not* from New York City but from Pittsburgh, and that she would *not* be going home anytime soon. Emma blushed a deep red, while the other kids fought to stifle laughs. Why Mrs. Walsh enjoyed being mean no one really knew, but she did and that was a fact. So it was no wonder that they were all happy when she left them alone to get on with the rehearsal.

Now Coach Cullimore, who was also the math teacher, was perfectly capable of being a shortstop or doing long division, but he could not, as his dear old mother use to say, carry a tune in a bucket. Nor could he play the piano, which became obvious after just a few notes. The students cringed.

"I think it's more like this," Mike suggested, as something more closely resembling music came from the piano.

"You're in!" Coach directed. "You can take the position at the piano from here on out."

"No, no, no," Mike protested, head shaking. "My mom forced me to take lessons, but I never practiced. I really can't play. But my mom, now, she's great on the piano!"

"Really?! Do you think she would be willing to come play for us?" the coach asked Mike.

"Well, not if *I* ask her," Mike said in a knowing manner. "But maybe if you asked her personally . . ." Mike really liked the coach and knew his mom would too.

Emma was to be the Partridge in a Pear Tree, and found herself sticking her head through a hole in a large cardboard painting of a pear tree. This was her second embarrassment of the day—not something an adventure hero should be doing. Unless, of course, that adventure hero was working undercover. That thought helped Emma get through the rehearsal and the rest of the day until school let out and she could go look for that job she promised Dolores she would find.

Naturally Emma first went to the town newspaper to offer her services as a paper "boy." But this was the *Doverville Trumpet* not the *Pittsburgh Herald*, and the editor of the paper himself doubled as the paper "boy." She went to the general store and the hardware store, to the dry goods store and to the butcher; but no one had a job for an adult, much less a kid, much less a girl kid, as several of the boys from her class were happy to tell her. But they also told her about Old Jake down by the river; he always had chores for kids. "Really?" Emma asked. "Yeah, just follow the river to the old bridge. It'll be right there." Emma thanked the boys and set off with renewed hope. One of the boys yelled after her, "It's a ways, but it's worth it!" But she did not hear him then say to his companions, "Yeah, if you like being eaten by dogs," which his friends thought was a pretty funny idea.

Emma tramped though the snow alongside the river for a quite a long way. She passed the time in three separate triumphant adventures, all taking place in her head, but they seemed pretty real nonetheless. Just when she thought she might be lost—which would have been a real and maybe not-so-fun adventure—she saw the old bridge, and there, close to it, was a rundown barn in the yard behind a tumbled-down fence with a crude, handwritten sign on it that read: KEEP OUT. There was a sign on the barn that said: WARNING DOGS BITE—HARD.

Well, Emma thought, *after coming all this way, I can't stop now.* Emma opened the gate and entered the yard, which, when the growling started, she thought might just have been a mistake. But there was no turning back now, as a large German Shepherd growling through bared teeth stood in her way. The

Shepherd was followed by a snow white Husky that came out of a doghouse and gave her an accusing look. Barks, howls, growls, and yaps filled the air as she found herself surrounded by big dogs with, she assumed, big appetites. Then from out of the shadow of the barn came a large presence, all bundled up with a furry head and a gray beard.

"The signs aren't big enough for you?" boomed the voice of Old Jake, the man who had rescued her the other day. "Just because I saved your hide don't mean I won't let the dogs eat you!"

Emma was scared, but not scared enough to back down. "I'm looking for a job."

"Those bully boys send you way out here?" Old Jake asked as he started throwing food scraps from a bucket to the dogs, which happily tussled over them.

"Yes, sir."

"Ahhhgg. They need a good thrashing, those hoodlums."

"I can work every day after school."

"I'm not used to having kids working here. I hate kids—mostly. So do the dogs—usually." Old Jake did not really smile at Emma, but his eyes looked as if he had. Then he threw some more scraps out. "They love the scraps; it makes 'em think they're people."

Old Jake had no job for Emma, but he offered to

take her home on his dog sled. She gratefully accepted the ride, but asked if he could take her to the Stevens farm so she could pick up the puppy instead. She knew that Mrs. Stevens would be happy to take her home from there.

9

Puppy Trouble

Late that night Emma wrote her dad a letter. She had no idea where to mail it, but it made her feel good to "talk" to him about her adventures in Doverville, about Mrs. Stevens and Mike, about the puppy, about the awful dogcatcher Doyle, about Old Jake, who was really nice despite his rough exterior, about the Christmas program, which she was not looking forward to, and about his coming by Christmas, which she was. She did not mention Dolores being less than welcoming, nor how mean Mrs. Walsh could be, because adventure heroes don't complain.

While she was occupied with the letter, the puppy snuck out of her room and padded his way down the stairs and into Dolores's salon. It is often said that cats are curious, but no more so than puppies, and the salon had so many things in it to be curious about. There were boxes of powder and bottles of liquid, there were hair rollers and face cream, there were tabletops to jump on full of interesting things to knock off, and, best of all, there were ladies' wigs that perched like fine creatures to attack—just like cats, which they sort of resembled.

Emma became aware of a growing clatter downstairs and the puppy's absence upstairs at just about the same time. "Oh my goodness!" she gasped, bounding from her room and down the stairs as quietly as possible, hoping not to wake Dolores. She found the puppy in the salon and the salon in a mess. Emma had no time to figure out what to do, for suddenly she was startled by a figure in the doorway: Dolores in a nightgown, robe, hair curlers, and face cream. But even more startling was the bloodcurdling scream that erupted from that ghostly white face.

"He was just looking for something to eat," Emma quickly explained, but Dolores was unresponsive. Emma was not even sure she had noticed the puppy. "I'm sorry," Emma tried again. "I'll clean it up."

Dolores opened her mouth to speak, but nothing came. She took a breath, stuttered something incomprehensible, and took another gasp of air before she could manage to say, "Do not . . . touch . . . anything.

Y-you go straight to your room and take that—What is that?! Is that a dog?!" Emma ran from the salon and started upstairs. "Well, take—take it with you!" Dolores shouted after her. "And tomorrow I'm going to find you another place to live!"

Emma felt horrible. It was wrong what the puppy did, and the puppy had been her responsibility. She wished it had never happened, but she knew this wish could not be granted. And the puppy was still hungry. Emma waited until she was pretty sure Dolores had gone to bed, then she quietly carried the puppy downstairs. In the kitchen she found the puppy some food, then she went into the salon. It was still a mess—obviously Dolores could not face cleaning it up so late. Emma remembered her offer and knew what she had to do. It was her mess, and every good adventure hero cleans up her own messes.

The next morning Dolores came downstairs hoping the horror of the night before had just been a bad dream. And when she looked into the salon, she thought it just might have been. The salon was now immaculately clean and orderly, and she believed it even sparkled. But it hadn't been a dream. *Poor kid,* she thought. *She must have worked all night.* She went upstairs to thank Emma, but Emma was deeply asleep, the puppy in her arms. *Well,* Dolores considered, *if Douglas O'Connor has raised this child alone, he hasn't done such a bad job.* The thought confused her, for the Douglas she remembered had been— A knock on the door downstairs interrupted her memory. *Who could that be?* It was still too early for a customer. She ran downstairs and opened the door to be greeted by one of the most horrible sights she had ever seen in her entire life: Norman Doyle with a silly grin on his face holding a sprig of mistletoe over his shaggy head.

Emma never knew how valiantly Dolores had worked to entice Norman into her salon for a free haircut and a shave while keeping him and his mistletoe at arm's length, especially when his mangy cat, old Scratch, started smelling the puppy, making Norman very suspicious. If Emma had witnessed the scene, she might have realized that Dolores was having a change of heart, and she might not have asked Mrs. Stevens if she and the puppy could stay with her from now on, as her "Aunt" Dolores wasn't feeling too well. But all Emma knew was that loud voices had woken her up, and Dolores had yelled something about how a nice haircut and shave would take Norman's mind off "CATCHING ALL THOSE DOGS!" So Emma had dressed quickly and slipped the puppy out of the house while Norman sat in the salon with a hot towel covering his face.

"Of course you can stay with us, Emma," Mrs. Stevens said. "I'll call Dolores about it later."

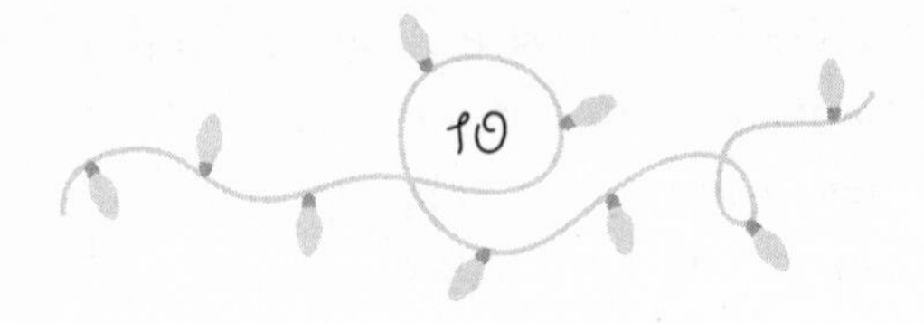

Shack Attack

Mayor Nobel Doyle had never really liked Cathy Stevens. It probably went back to when they were children and Cathy had called him "Stinky" and his brother "Dirty Doyle," even though they were the grandchildren of one of the founders of Doverville. But that was a long time ago, and now there were far more recent reasons for him not to like her. Cathy had been a thorn in his side about the whole dog question, taking in all the dogs he was trying to get rid of, and getting major national publicity for it in *LIKE* magazine in an article that did not even mention him by name but simply called him "the dog-hating mayor of Doverville." It had always been his dream to get his name in a national magazine.

But there was nothing the mayor could do about Cathy, for she lived outside of the city limits.

"Well, why don't you just move those darn city limits past her farm then," his brother suggested in all his brilliance.

"Brilliant!" the mayor declared. And he told the Town Council to make it so.

It was with great pleasure that Mayor Doyle drove himself out to just beyond the Stevens farm to plant the new city limits sign. He then went to visit Cathy Stevens, who had been watching him from the barn.

"To what do we owe the 'honor,' Your Honor?" Mrs. Stevens asked when the mayor got out of his fancy car.

"Mrs. Stevens, I can appreciate that living out of town all these years has deprived you of any real sense of community, which is a real shame. But our town is growing, you might say, and I came out here to officially welcome you to Doverville." The mayor smiled pleasantly. But Mrs. Stevens knew it was only a sneer in disguise. "That means, of course, the dogs will have to go."

"It takes more than moving a sign to change a town, *Stinky.* The dogs are not going anywhere, and neither am I!"

CHAPTER 10

Upon hearing his old nickname, the mayor's smile dropped its disguise. "The dogs *will* go, Mrs. Stevens. For their sake I hope you're not as foolish as you sound."

As the mayor's car drove away, Cathy Stevens marched across the snow-covered field to the edge of the road, pulled the city limits sign out of the ground, and tossed it away.

Max wondered why they seemed upset—the kids and the nice lady. The nice lady had been outside of the barn talking to someone who had a voice that Max did not like at all. Maybe that's why they were upset. But now the lady was in the barn.

"Any luck?" the lady said to the kids.

"No," the girl said. "Max still won't come out of the doghouse."

"Mom," the boy questioned, "can Mayor Doyle really take the dogs?"

"I don't know, Mike. I know he's going to try, but how, I don't know. He's only got a one-man police force and his brother to help him. Still, we better be on our guard."

"It's like a war then," the boy said, worried.

"Well, honey, 'war' may be too strong a word."

But "war" wasn't too strong a word for Nobel and Norman Doyle. War is exactly how they thought of their campaign to drive out the dogs. Mrs. Stevens started feeling the effects of that campaign almost immediately when she went into town to get food for the dogs. First, there was Ralph at the general store, who told her that he just wasn't stocking dog kibbles anymore. Then there was John, the butcher who had always given her the trims from the meat, but now he refused. And others in the town were suddenly just as uncooperative. It was then that Mrs. Stevens knew this was serious. New orphan dogs were coming in every week, new mouths to feed, and Mrs. Stevens now didn't know where she was going to get the food.

She lay in bed that night worrying about it and did not fall asleep until the wee hours. Unfortunately it was in the wee hours that bug-face Melvin took a pair of wire cutters and cut a hole in her dog-yard fence.

The next morning, before leaving for school, Mike said good-bye to Yeti, and Emma said good-bye to the puppy, both expecting not to see their dogs again until after school. But it was not to be. The new hole in the fence, which no one had noticed, allowed Yeti and the puppy to happily run after Mrs. Stevens's truck, eventually making it into town and to the school.

Class started that morning with spelling, which Mrs. Walsh, who had reluctantly taken over Mrs. Clancy's class, was testing the students on. She called first on Miranda, the smartest kid in the school, and asked her to spell *discipline,* Mrs. Walsh's favorite word.

Miranda, who was happy to have been called upon, stood up quickly and said, "Discipline, D-I-S-C-I-P-L-I-N-E." After defining the word she sat down pertly, for she knew she had spelled the word correctly.

"Good, very good," Mrs. Walsh said as she looked for her next "volunteer." It did not take her long to decide, turning to Emma and asking her to spell *prevarication.* Emma stood up and was about to do so when Yeti casually walked into the classroom, just as if she belonged there, followed by the puppy, leaping and bouncing about, eventually leaping into Emma's arms. This canine invasion shocked Mrs. Walsh, but delighted the kids. Mrs. Walsh got over her shock quickly, though, and, disgusted, grabbed Yeti by the collar and escorted her out of the classroom. "Out-out-out!"

Mike and Emma ran to the window and soon saw

Mrs. Walsh dragging Yeti across the snow-covered schoolyard in her high-heeled shoes, then shooing her away. They couldn't help but laugh at the sight. Then they heard an awful noise. It was the warped putt-putt and occasional rude backfire of the Fearsome Machine, which could be seen coming around the corner. Bug-face Melvin was driving, and Norman Doyle was standing up in his seat vigilantly looking for criminal dogs, like Captain Ahab searching for Moby Dick. Mike and Emma knew they quickly had to go out and find Yeti and take her and the puppy, which was still in Emma's arms, and hide them. They grabbed their hats and coats and were just running out of the classroom when Mrs. Walsh returned. Mike dashed around her, but she blocked Emma's way, giving her a look that would have melted her like wax, had Emma not been an adventure hero.

"Prevarication, P-R-E-V—uh, it's a deviation from the truth," Emma said as she attempted to move past the principal, but Mrs. Walsh grabbed her by the arm.

"Did you bring that dog to school?" she demanded to know.

"What dog?" Emma said with innocent eyes while holding the puppy close. Mrs. Walsh was so taken aback by this prevarication, she let go of Emma, who then ran from the classroom.

CHAPTER 10

Mike and Emma had exactly the same idea, and they took the dogs to the large storage shack at the rear of the school, hiding themselves deep in the darkness. But it was too obvious a choice, for bug-face Melvin and Norman soon rode up on the Fearsome Machine, stopping right in front of the shack's door.

Emma turned to Mike. "You hide; I'll distract Norman." Just as Norman, with old dog-sniffing Scratch in his arms, came into the shack, Emma bolted out of the shadows and headed deeper into the shack, into a back room where she found a stack of long corrugated metal culverts of various sizes, including one that was just right for a girl and her dog to hide in.

Emma put the puppy into the big tube and was just climbing in after him, when she heard the door of the room slam, then Norman thumping around, and then old Scratch letting out a threatening yowl. "You caused me a lot of trouble, but you're not getting out of this one," Norman said. Emma held the puppy tight and her breath still, hoping Norman would not think to look in the culverts. Unfortunately she could not stop scent, and soon old Scratch found them out. Norman's shaggy head appeared at the end of the culvert, grinning in triumph. "Look what I have, puppy," he said, holding out his cat as a tempting treat. Emma tried to keep the puppy from running, but a cat is a cat, and puppies chase cats, and that's all there is to it. The puppy broke Emma's grip and soon found himself in Norman's welcoming, though not very loving, arms.

By the time Emma got herself out of the culvert and out of the shack, the Fearsome Machine was driving away, with Yeti locked into the dog cage and the puppy bouncing around in a dog net hanging off the back.

"Emma," came a plea from behind her. She turned around and saw Mike hanging by his coat high on a hook on the wall inside the shack. "Get me down," he said as he struggled like a worm. Had they not just lost their dogs to bug-face Melvin and Dogcatcher Doyle, it might have been a very funny sight.

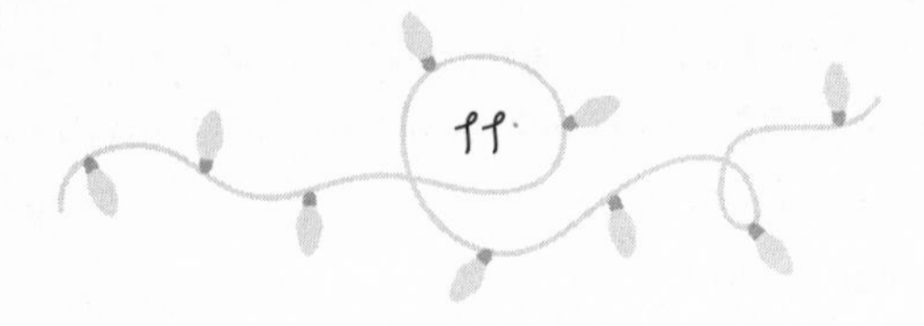

Emma Undercover

Coach Cullimore had moved to Doverville several months before when he had gotten his job at the school, a job he knew he was lucky to have. Of the one hundred schools he had applied to, eighty-nine wrote back that they were no longer hiring due to the Depression, and ten wrote that they had already given their jobs to teachers with more experience. He had grown rather discouraged when he got the letter from Mrs. Walsh offering him the coaching job if he could also teach math. Although Maine was a state he had never thought he would want to live in, he snapped up the job, and now was very glad he did. Maine was beautiful, and he realized after a couple of months that he just might want to live there for the rest of his life. He was thinking that very thought as he was driving his car along the Old River Road looking for the Stevens farm.

"Excuse me," he said to an attractive woman standing by a group of mailboxes on the road. "Can you tell me where 209 is?"

As that was her address, Cathy Stevens was a little suspicious of this stranger. "Who you looking for?"

"Mike Stevens. I'm Denton Cullimore from the school. Actually I'm looking for his mother, the, uh, the Dog Lady," he said, trying to be an "in the know" member of the community.

Cathy, who had been in town getting newly arrived dogs from the train station and had just stopped to pick up her mail, said, "The Dog Lady? Now why would a respectable teacher want to meet that crazy woman?"

"So it's true what they say about her in town?"

"Oh," Cathy answered with a very serious look on her face, "much worse, I'm afraid." She enjoyed "warning" the coach, whom Mike talked about incessantly. But since he said he wanted to meet Mrs. Stevens, she pointed out her farm, which was just behind him. The coach thanked this kind "stranger" and drove to the farm. Cathy waited a few minutes, and then followed him in her truck.

"So you're . . . ," Coach began when Cathy got out of her truck and started to unload the dogs.

"Cathy Stevens, the 'Crazy Dog Lady,'" she finished his sentence with a smile.

"Hey, I'm so sorry. I didn't . . ."

"You're not the first to think I lost my marbles. However, you are the first to want to meet me," Cathy said, remembering back to the days when she flirted with boys.

"See, they put me in charge of the Christmas program, and—"

"You want me to play the piano." Coach dropped his jaw a little. "Mikey mentioned it," Cathy continued. "But I'm afraid I can't. As you can see," she said, pointing to all the dogs, old and newly arrived, "this is a lot more than I bargained for. It's getting hard to keep up. But I can't bear the thought of even one of them going hungry. I just worry that I can't finish what I started."

The coach looked at Cathy and realized that maybe she was crazy—but only in an insanely generous sort of way. And Coach admired that kind of crazy. "You need help," he said feeling inspired. "I'll make a deal with you. You come play the piano for the program, and the kids and I will help you find food for the dogs."

Cathy laughed off the suggestion at first, but the coach was insistent. Maybe everything Mike had been telling her was true. The coach certainly was the only other adult who had offered to help. She warmed at the thought of a new helper and friend.

"Let me think about it, okay?"

"Okay!" the coach said, filled with hope.

When Dolores had received the call from Cathy Stevens telling her that she would be happy to have Emma stay with her, Dolores heard two voices within her with two separate opinions. One said, *Good riddance, you're well rid of the brat!* But another one said, *Ah, Dolores, you're going to miss her, aren't you?* Dolores was still not sure which one to listen to when Emma showed up after school to get her things. The one voice made her say to Emma, pointing to her shoes, "You are making a mess. Mud!" But the other voice made her say, "Look, sweetie, I got to thinking about you staying with Mrs. Stevens, and, well . . ."

"Can you still get me that job with the dogcatcher?" Emma did not mean to be rude and cut Dolores off—but she had a plan.

"Well, you certainly don't have to pay me if you're staying with Mrs. Stevens."

"I *need* that job."

Dolores was impressed. Emma did want to pay her

own way in the world. "Well, okay. If I ask him, he will give you the job," she said with a smile Emma had never seen before—and one that Emma hoped she would see more often.

Mike had been inconsolable about Yeti's capture, and Emma was just angry—angry enough to want to do something about it. But what could a kid do? Emma then decided she couldn't be a kid right now; she had to be an adventure hero for real. However, an adventure hero knows when she is outnumbered, and knows when it is time to go undercover. That's when Emma knew she had to ask Dolores to get her that job with the dogcatcher.

Emma started working that afternoon. Norman and bug-face Melvin had set up the city's new "dog pound" in an old abandoned buggy-whip factory. Its vast interior provided plenty of room for all the criminal dogs, which they kept in all manner of makeshift cages. They had covered the floor with hay to catch the dog "doody" that Norman hated so much, and they fed them very little, which kept them hungry, which Norman, for a particular reason, thought was a good thing. But it did mean that they whimpered a lot, and that got on Norman's nerves.

After Norman had told her what to do, which entailed a lot of lifting and carting and cleaning, he went into his "office," a room in the back. Emma took the opportunity to look around. The sight of all the dogs, whimpering in cages, just about broke her heart. But she couldn't help them all. Right now she had to find Yeti and the puppy, for she had promised Mike she would. After searching what seemed like hundreds of cages, she finally came across the one that contained Yeti. And next to it was a small cage with the puppy in it. She petted them both and whispered, "Don't you worry. I'll get you all out of here soon." She was just trying to figure out how to unlock the cages when, suddenly, a greasy-gloved hand grabbed her braids and pulled her away from the cages.

"I told Dolores that hiring a girl would be stupid," Norman said into Emma's face, his hot, stinky breath making her cringe more than the pain of having her hair pulled. "But then I discovered that the girl was the dog-loving, trouble-making girl, and I thought that it would be good to have her right here with me, so I could keep my eye on her." He pointed a grimy finger at her nose. "You remember that as far as I'm concerned, you're no better than another stray dog. Now get back to work!" Norman pushed Emma away from Yeti and the puppy, and the puppy growled at him, and Norman growled right back.

That night, Norman made Emma work late, and she got back to the Stevens farm after Mike had gone to bed, so she was not able to report on her undercover work. In the morning Mrs. Stevens didn't have the heart to wake her early, so she drove Mike to school, then drove back to get Emma.

At the school Coach Cullimore was giving it his all in rehearsing the kids in "The Twelve Days of Christmas." He plotted out their moves on a blackboard like he would football plays, and tried in his tone-deaf way to lead them in singing. Neither effort was succeeding—which Mrs. Stevens could plainly see as she and Emma entered the assembly hall. The coach did not see her enter, so it was the most pleasant of surprises when suddenly, instead of the off-key caterwauling he was leading, there was music, sweet music, as Mrs. Stevens started playing the piano, and the kids started singing in tune.

"That was great!" the coach said when the song had been successfully sung. "We have been saved by Mike's mom!" he announced to the kids with great relief.

Emma had made her way up to the stage, and Mike approached her anxiously. "Did you find Yeti?" Mike asked. Emma told him that she had, but she had not been able to rescue them. "But we have got to get them out of there!" Mike said loudly just as Coach was trying to organize one more go at the song.

"Em and Mike, come on, you're holding up the game."

Mrs. Stevens started playing again, and Emma grabbed her cardboard partridge tree. "You got to get her out of there fast." The conversation continued behind the cardboard.

"I will," Emma assured.

"Promise?" Mike pleaded.

"I promise," Emma declared like the stalwart adventure hero she was determined to be.

After the rehearsal, Coach stepped over to the piano. "See, I told you your piano playing would make all the difference." Mrs. Stevens smiled at the compliment. "You know, it's really nice of you to help us out like this," he continued. "Thanks."

"You're welcome," Mrs. Stevens said. "Anything to feed the dogs."

Ah, yes, the dogs, the coach thought. *How are we going to help the dogs?*

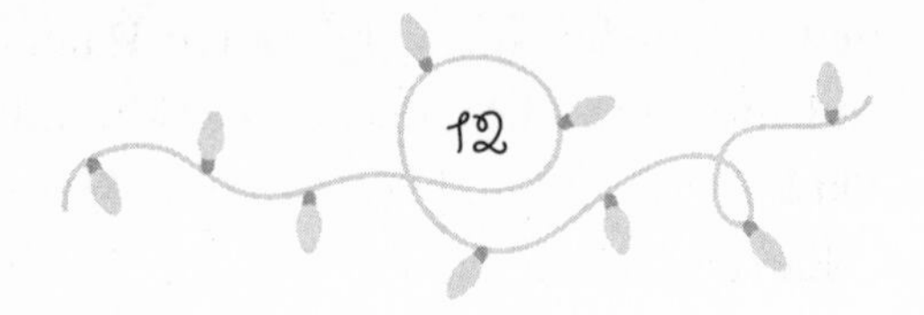

Caught!

In the few months he had been in Doverville, Coach had grown quite fond of his students. They were an enthusiastic bunch, but more importantly, they were a positive bunch. Times were hard, yet they kept up their spirits. Some of that is natural to children, but he was convinced that his kids were special. So, in order to solve the dog-feeding dilemma, he gathered his students at the Stevens farm and put a question to them.

"All right, kids, I have your math assignment. Now, you remember how to do story problems, right? You've got a basket with ten apples in it. You take two out. How many are left?"

"Eight," one of the kids answered.

"Right. Well, now, just think dogs. How many do we have, Mikey?"

Mike started counting the dogs in the yard. "Okay, so we got . . . four Cocker Spaniels, ten Dalmatians, and seven Chihuahuas." As he counted, Miranda, the smartest kid in the school, kept a running total. "We got five Retrievers and seven Boxers, five Basset Hounds, two black Labradors, and nine Lab puppies."

"And Max," Mrs. Stevens said.

"And a Poodle in a doghouse," Mike finished up, but then remembered something and turned to the coach. "And you have to count Yeti and the puppy, because Emma's going to get them back."

Max was curious. There was so much going on outside of the barn. He heard the voices of many children, but they weren't quite the voices of play. There was something more serious about their voices. Max started to leave his doghouse. He so much wanted to see what was going on, but he stopped. No! There was no voice of Mr. Whiteside; he would only leave for the voice of Mr. Whiteside.

"Okay," the coach said. "So how many kids, how many dogs, and how many meals for each of us to find?"

CHAPTER 12

Miranda, after some swift calculations on an abacus, proudly announced the answer. "There are twenty-eight pupils, plus Coach Cullimore and Mrs. Stevens. There are fifty-two dogs, but you can't really count Yeti and the puppy until Emma actually brings them back. Each dog eats twice a day, so that means each of us must provide three and six-tenths meals per day."

But exactly how were they to do that? Mrs. Stevens looked to Coach Cullimore; Coach Cullimore looked to the students; the students looked to Mrs. Stevens. No one had an answer—until Emma spoke up.

"Do you guys ever collect bacon grease around here?" They all looked at Emma, totally perplexed. "I used to collect cans of bacon grease from the neighbors once a week to sell to make soap."

"Dogs can't live off bacon grease," Mike rightly said.

"No," Emma said confidently because she knew the solution. "But they love table scraps—makes them think they're people. The sign says there are 887 people living in Doverville. If half that many gives us scraps, that's . . ."

"Four hundred fourty-four, rounded up," Miranda announced.

"Uh, that's optimistic," Mrs. Stevens cautioned.

"But even half that many . . ." Emma was determined.

"Two hundred twenty-three," Miranda calculated.

That sounded a bit more realistic. "Well," Coach said, "scraps are thrown out anyway."

"I used to collect *a lot* of bacon grease," Emma added.

"That's only seven and a half houses per person per week," Miranda the math wiz said.

"How can you visit half a house?" Mike wanted to know.

Despite that, everyone was enthusiastic over the plan and was just signing up to do their bit, when they heard the warped *putt-putt* and rude backfires of the Fearsome Machine, which drove up fast and came to an abrupt stop.

"Merry Christmas, dog lovers, merry Christmas!" Norman shouted out as he dismounted from his high seat with a piece of paper, a nail, and a hammer in his hand. He marched over to the side of the barn and nailed the paper to it. It was a notice that read: BY ORDER OF THE MAYOR, ALL DOGS MUST BE REMOVED ON OR BEFORE MIDNIGHT DECEMBER 24. "A little extra time, Mrs. Stevens, in the spirit of the season." He chuckled an unpleasant chuckle. "But I can assure you if those dogs are still here on Christmas Day, they are mine!" Then he spotted Emma. "There you are." He walked over to Emma and grabbed her by one of her braids. "Come on, you're late for work." He dragged Emma toward the Fearsome Machine. Mrs. Stevens rushed to stop him, but Mike stopped her and reminded her that Emma working for Norman was their only hope of getting Yeti back.

Norman gave Emma the task of cleaning out all the cages. Emma wanted to feed the dogs, but Norman said they had already been fed. If they had, it hadn't been much, and many of the dogs whimpered with hunger. "Keep them quiet," Norman ordered. "That's part of your job, too, to keep them mangy mutts quiet."

Emma kept hoping Norman would leave or go in his office, but he stayed close and kept an eye on her. The advantage was that she could also keep an eye on Norman, and she soon learned where he kept a large ring of keys, the keys to the various dog cage padlocks. Norman had used one of the keys to open a cage and take out a Border Collie, which he then dragged away. Emma put down her cleaning tools and quietly followed him, seeing where he hooked the key ring on a nail in the office before going out again to help bug-face Melvin put the Collie into another cage by the front. Emma went into the office to get the keys, keeping an eye through the door on the two men. Suddenly old Scratch jumped on top of the old metal filing cabinet Emma was standing by, meowing an alarm. Quickly, Emma opened the top drawer and pushed old Scratch in, then closed it. Then she grabbed the keys and ran out of the office.

She made her way to the puppy's cage and opened it, took him out, and held him tight. Then she turned to Yeti's cage, but the cage door was already opened, and Yeti was gone. The surrounding dogs were getting excited and starting to bark. "Hey," she heard Norman yell from a distance, "I told you to keep them dogs from yapping! Shut them up!" But Emma had moved to the back of the old factory and found another room to hide in.

Norman, growing suspicious, started to look for her. "Bad things happen to bad little girls—you hear me?! Where are you?" Then he came upon the puppy's empty cage. "Ho, ho, you have gone and done it now." He called bug-face Melvin over, and Emma could see from a crack in the door that they were plotting something horrible. She decided to move farther back into the room, and there she discovered something strange. On a roll of hooks dangled dog collars, a lot of dog collars! Why were they here? Why weren't they on the dogs? And where were the dogs they belonged to? Emma got a sinking feeling. What had bug-face Melvin and Norman been doing with the dogs? And then she saw that one collar had a name marked on it in ink: YETI. Right then and there Emma knew that she could not just rescue the puppy; she had to rescue all the dogs!

Emma looked back into the main part of the dog pound and didn't see Norman anywhere. She went in and started opening up all the cages with Norman's keys, releasing Labs and Collies, Retrievers and German Shepherds, then she herded them to a big side door.

As soon as she opened the door, she was hit in the face with a bright light. It was the headlamps of a truck. She squinted to see bug-face Melvin scurrying to gather the newly freed dogs. Then a hand, a greasy-gloved hand, came down on her shoulder from behind her, and she heard the faint cackling of Norman Doyle's voice and smelled the less-than-faint scent of his breath.

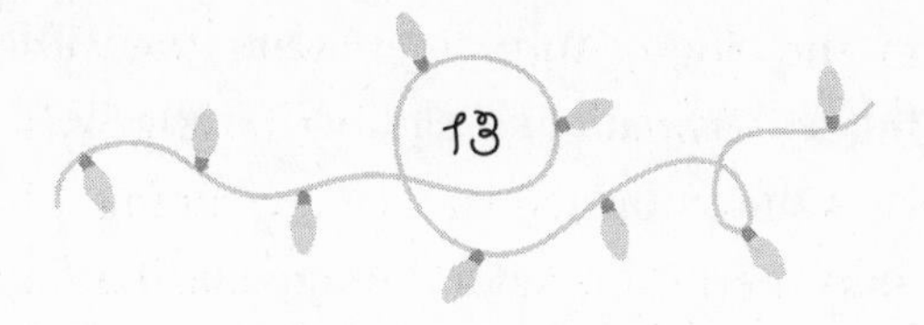

13

Dolores to the Rescue

The next day was Saturday, but all the kids had agreed to come to school in the morning for another rehearsal of the Christmas program. Afterward they would go out to collect table scraps for the dogs. When Mrs. Stevens and Mike got up that morning, they found that Emma was not in her bed. They thought that maybe Norman had made her work late again and she had decided to stay in town with Dolores. They figured they would see her at the rehearsal.

As Mike and his mother were driving into town, they saw several dogs running in the street. They looked at one another. "Emma!" they shouted. "She must have let them out of the dog pound." Mrs. Stevens explained what they both were thinking.

CHAPTER 13

They stopped the truck and scrambled to round up the dogs, managing to get seven of them into the truck. But Yeti was not among them. And where were Emma and the puppy?

When Mrs. Stevens and Mike came into the assembly hall, Coach and the kids were in the middle of rehearsing the moves the coach had worked out on the blackboard. Girls with flutes were playing pipers, and boys with gold foil cardboard rings were holding them up high; other boys were leaping like lords, while a few girls were making the motions of milking cows. The coach had not yet figured out how he would indicate geese laying eggs. None of this was poetry in motion, and on top of that, their partridge in a pear tree, Emma, was not there.

"Sorry we're late," Mrs. Stevens said as Mike ran to the stage and she positioned herself on the piano bench. "But something came up that was really worth being late for."

"Where's Emma?" Coach Cullimore asked.

"She didn't come to school?"

The coach shook his head no and exchanged a worried glance with Mrs. Stevens. But they knew how independent Emma was. Besides, they had a rehearsal to finish, and over fifty dogs to feed.

Had they known where Emma was, though, they

would have dropped everything and rushed to her rescue. Emma was crouched in a cold corner of the old buggy-whip factory, locked into a large cage with only her puppy to keep her warm.

After the rehearsal Coach Cullimore drove half the kids to one end of the town, and Mrs. Stevens drove the other half to the other end so the kids could start knocking on doors collecting scraps for the dogs. The excitement over their mission was quickly extinguished, as the kids experienced one door slam after another. The residents of the town dismissed them as pesky beggars.

Then Miranda, who, as you know, was the smartest kid in the school, got an idea. "Look," she said to the other kids in a huddle, "we've been rehearsing Christmas carols for days. Why not give them something for what we're asking? Grown-ups love that stuff!"

The next time they knocked on a door, the man answering it, roast beef sandwich in hand, was greeted by a choir of kids singing "Gloria" as backup to Mike's sterling performance as "Tiny Tim" complete with crutch. "Kind sir," Mike began, "it's Christmas. Our dogs are very hungry. They're good little fellows, they are. In the kindness of your heart, could you spare a little something left over from your lovely dinner?" The man thought for a moment. About what we can have no idea. But whatever his thoughts were, they turned to kindness, and he placed his sandwich in the bucket Mike offered up. This same gesture was repeated over and over throughout the rest of the day, including at the butcher's, which made John the butcher feel better than he had felt in many days.

When the kids got to the Stevens farm that afternoon, they had plenty of food for the dogs. Mrs. Stevens was thrilled. But they still had not heard from Emma, and Mrs. Stevens was worried. She called Dolores to see if Emma had spent the night there, but Dolores said no, she had not seen her. But she also told Mrs. Stevens not to worry, for she had a pretty good idea where Emma might be.

Angry and determined, Dolores grabbed her hat and coat and drove her old Model T Ford to the abandoned buggy-whip factory and confronted Norman, her "boyfriend."

"I don't know what you're so sore about, Dolores." Norman ran after her as Dolores made her way through the building, looking for Emma. "I was just trying to teach her a lesson."

"Where is she, Norman?!"

"Around the corner."

And around the corner Dolores found Emma. "A cage?!" She ran up to Emma. "Did they hurt you?"

Dolores ordered Norman to open the cage, which he reluctantly did. "Come on, honey, I told you it was a stupid idea to give a girl a job like this. She let all the dogs out!"

"I'm not listening to you, Norman," Dolores said as she walked Emma and the puppy out of the factory.

Norman grabbed Emma away from Dolores just as they were leaving. "All right, now, that is enough! I know what's going on here. Oh, yeah, you want a favor, then it's all sweet talk and perfume and *oo-la-la*, and all the time this ragamuffin kid's more important to you than I am. Well, the kid is fired, and the dumb mutt stays here."

Dolores had never really hit a man before. She did not consider it ladylike. But she smacked Norman good on his arm, and in shock and pain Norman let go of Emma.

"We are through, Dolores!" Norman yelled after her as she took Emma and the puppy to her car.

"Fine!" Dolores yelled back.

"I mean it!" Norman emphasized.

"Wonderful!" Dolores was happy to agree.

"Thanks for getting me out, Aunt Dolores," Emma said at the car.

"Do *not* call me that! I could crack your daddy's skull for—"

"It's not his fault that I'm so much trouble."

"Trouble? You are ruining my life," Dolores corrected. But did she mean it? She suddenly looked at Emma, reached into her pocket, and pulled out an envelope. "Your daddy's letter finally got here. Why didn't you tell me what happened to your mother?" Emma had no answer, for she did not like to talk about her mother's death. "Look, I don't know what your daddy told you about me—about us—but, well, a long time ago I knew your daddy real well, and all I can say is you just better not go depending on what he says because even when he makes a promise it's not something you can trust." Dolores could see that this was hurting Emma, but Emma, she figured, needed to know, so she wouldn't be hurt anymore. "I'm just saying he is not likely to be here by Christmas—or ever, for that matter. Now, get in!"

They drove in silence except when Dolores offered to let Emma stay with her again. She was hoping Emma would say yes, but Emma wanted to keep the puppy, and she couldn't do that at Dolores's because, despite what Norman had said, they both knew he would be coming around.

Dolores drove Emma to the Stevens farm. When Emma started to get out of the car, Dolores handed her a bundle. "I brought you a few things."

They were clothes—girl's clothes—and a nice girl's coat and a pair of girl's shoes. Where did they come from? Had there been another young girl in Dolores's past? Or had she actually spent her own money and bought them? Or taken her own time and made the dresses? She wasn't saying; she was just smiling at this daughter of a man who had once been important to her. "If you ever wanted to come by," Dolores offered as Emma held the clothes tightly with wide eyes, "I would love to do something about that hair. Okay?"

"Okay," Emma said, thinking how nice that might be. "And thank you for . . . for everything."

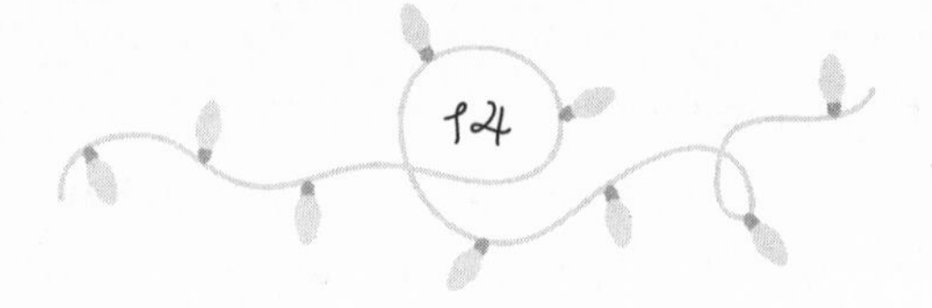

Emma to the Rescue

Max, sitting in his doghouse, watched the girl in the cap walk into the barn carrying a big bundle, which did not interest Max, and her puppy, which did. Maybe the puppy would come over to him and he could sniff the puppy, see where the puppy had been. That would be nice. Unfortunately, the boy came running in, and the girl put the puppy down by him. Seeing that the boy was upset, the puppy went in the opposite direction. The boy, near tears, asked about Yeti. Max remembered Yeti. She was the good-looking Sheepdog who had smelled really nice. Max hadn't seen her for a while and had wondered where she had gone. The girl took something out of her pocket and showed it to the boy. Max recognized it; it was Yeti's collar. A tear rolled down the boy's cheek. "But where is she now?" he asked. "You said she was there; why didn't you let her out?" The girl tried to explain,

Emma (Jordan-Claire Green) on the train

Cathy Stevens (Susan Wood) and her son, Mike (Adam Hicks), help unload dogs

Emma comes to Doverville

Mabel (Dorothy Brodesser) and "Aunt" Dolores (Bonita Friedericy) in the salon

Mrs. Walsh (Mindy Sterling) confronts Emma

The two Emmas: Emma Kragen, the author of the picture book, *The Twelve Dogs of Christmas* and Emma O'Connor, the character

Coach Cullimore (Eric Lutes) attempting to play the piano as Mike watches

Dogcatcher Norman Doyle (John Billingsley) and his dog-sniffing cat, Scratch

Coach Cullimore looking for "The Dog Lady"

Cathy Stevens, "The Dog Lady"

Director Kieth Merrill

The Mayor's Mansion ready for the Christmas party

The dogs at Dolores's shop, preparing for the show

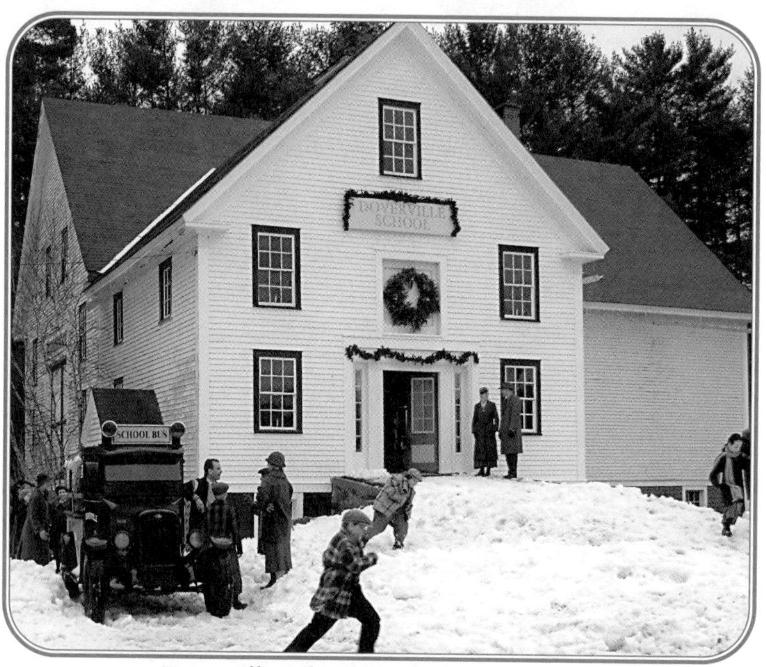

Doverville School just before the show

The musical finale . . .

And a poodle in a doghouse!

Mayor Doyle (Richard Reihle) dedicating the city's new dog orphanage

but the boy was too upset to listen. "You lied to me!" "I didn't lie." "Yes, you did! Did they kill her?" The girl in the cap seemed to have no answer. "No—no, you let them kill her! You lied to me, Emma! You never tell the truth! You lied. You said you're from New York, and you're not. And you said you have a mother, and you don't! And I bet your father's not coming for you either! You're probably just a runaway girl and don't even have a father!" The boy then ran out of the barn, crying loudly. Max looked at the girl and recognized the sadness in her eyes because he had felt so sad himself.

Something had to be done. That Emma knew. Maybe it was a war after all, and Emma, the adventure hero, had to take action. Mike had depended on her, and she had failed him. She would not fail him again. She decided to take a bold action, and late that night after Mrs. Stevens and Mike had gone to bed, she quietly left the house. She needed to get to the old buggy-whip factory quickly, so she decided to borrow Mrs. Stevens's flatbed truck.

Emma's father, who for a short time had gotten a truck-driving job, had taught her to drive, so she knew exactly what to do, even if she had to stretch her legs a lot to reach the pedals. Still, it would beat walking through the woods on the cold winter's night.

The old buggy-whip factory was at the edge of the woods, and as Emma got closer she noticed some strange lights off among the trees. Some, she could tell, were headlamps from cars and trucks; some flickered as if there were a campfire. Maybe that was it—maybe it was a Boy Scout camp or something. But why would Boy Scouts go camping in winter? Normally, as an adventure hero, this was just the kind of mystery she would investigate, but she had no time to do so now.

As she got close to Norman's dog pound, she turned off the engine and coasted to a stop. She got out quietly and made her way into the old factory. There she saw Norman and bug-face Melvin loading a truck with dogs in cages. They loaded a Labrador, and then headed back into the main part of the building where all the dogs were. Why were they doing this? Where were they taking the dogs? It couldn't be anywhere good, Emma knew, not with Norman and Melvin involved.

Emma made a quick decision: the only way she was going to find out would be to ride along. So she took a deep breath and climbed into Norman's truck, hiding behind several dog cages.

"This dog stinks!" Emma heard Norman say as he and bug-face Melvin returned with another cage. "In fact, they all stink. Mangy, filthy mutts!" Emma ducked as a cage was pushed into the truck. Then the canvas flaps at the back of the truck were tied down, and Emma could hear Norman and Melvin climb into the cab.

It was not a long trip. The two men got out of the truck and walked away, Norman saying, "All right, let's go do some business." Emma carefully made her way around the cages and out of the back of the truck. She saw that she was by an old, run-down barn in the middle of the woods. She heard lots of voices of men talking and cheering and booing coming from the barn, as well as the agitated barking of dogs. There was a campfire outside of the barn, and some men were warming themselves by it. There were lots of cars and trucks parked nearby. This must be the place in the woods she saw! Emma resolved to go inside and find out what was going on. But first, she had to figure out how to get around the men by the campfire. And, more importantly, she better have a plan of escape. Her adventure heroes always had a good plan of escape. She looked all around. On the side of the barn, close to where bug-face Melvin had parked, was a long chain. She had no idea what it was for, but one end was attached securely to the barn, and that gave her an idea.

After preparing her plan of escape, Emma, by sliding through the shadows, made her way into the barn. There were many cages inside: some with dogs, some empty. Coming from deep within the barn, the sound of men and dogs was intense. As she got closer to the sound, she could hear dogs not just barking but growling. It was harsh, hate-filled growling, and it made Emma's heart pump fast and loud. Soon she saw a crowd of men formed into a circle looking down at the ground before them. They were shouting and yelling and throwing their fists up in the air. Some seemed happy; some seemed angry. Emma wanted to find out what they were watching, but the only way to do that would be to get above them. But how?

Emma looked around the barn and discovered the answer: a hayloft! She found the ladder to it and climbed up. From that vantage point she could see that the men were actually standing around a low fence shaped into a square, making a pen. There were two men within the pen, each holding a dog on a leash. One was a vicious looking German Shepherd. And the other—the other was Yeti! She still couldn't quite tell what they were going to do with them. She noticed that off to the side Norman and Melvin were collecting a bunch of money from a mean-looking, long-haired, bearded man who could have been straight from one of the Charles Dickens novels she had read at the library. She looked back down at the Shepherd and Yeti. They were being yelled at; they were being goaded. All the while the men around the fence were drinking from jugs and exchanging money. Bets! They were making bets! On a dogfight! Yeti! They were going to make sweet, gentle Yeti fight that vicious Shepherd! Emma knew she had to do something fast. Then she saw a hay hook on a long rope, and she thought of Robin Hood and Tarzan. She could swing down on the rope into the pen and rescue Yeti. *But the German Shepherd, the vicious Shepherd, what about him? Surprise . . . and luck,* she told herself. *I'm just going to have to depend on them.* She took a deep breath, grabbed the rope, and swung, and the betting men, the drinking and cheering and booing men, were truly surprised to see this hero in a cloth cap, her blonde braids flying behind her, land into the middle of the dogfight arena! "Give me that dog!" she demanded of the man holding Yeti's leash. The man looked at her as if she were not real, and certainly as if she were not a threat. He was corrected quickly in this assumption when Emma's foot slammed into his shin, causing him to buckle and drop the leash.

Emma grabbed it and ran with Yeti out of the pen, crashing through all the men who were too busy laughing at the man, who was now hopping on one leg, to stop her.

Emma ran. The old man with the beard was angry and was ready to take it out on Norman. Norman gave him assurances that he would get the dog back, then he and bug-face Melvin ran after Emma, all in the blink of the hundred glinting eyes of the betting men who thought it was all great fun.

When Norman and bug-face Melvin got to the truck, they could see Emma and Yeti running into the woods. "Get in the truck! We'll get her quick!" Norman yelled. But when they backed the truck out as fast as bug-face Melvin could go, they suddenly came to a jerking, jolting stop as the chain Emma had hooked to their front bumper came to the end of its length. "Arrguh! I hate that girl!" Norman screamed out for all the world to hear.

Emma knew exactly where she was and what direction to go. It took her very little time to make it back to the buggy-whip factory. She got Yeti into the cab of Mrs. Stevens's truck, then climbed in herself. On the drive back to the farm, her heart was still racing. Being an adventure hero sure was exciting. But it was dangerous too. And as brave as it made her feel, she was thinking she would like to wait a long time before she tried something like this again.

Back at the farm, Emma got Yeti into the barn and to her usual pen. She was then going to go to the house and go to bed, but the hay Yeti had laid down in looked so comfortable and inviting that Emma lay down next to the dog, who gave her a big lick of thanks. Emma put her arms around Yeti, and then fell into a deep sleep.

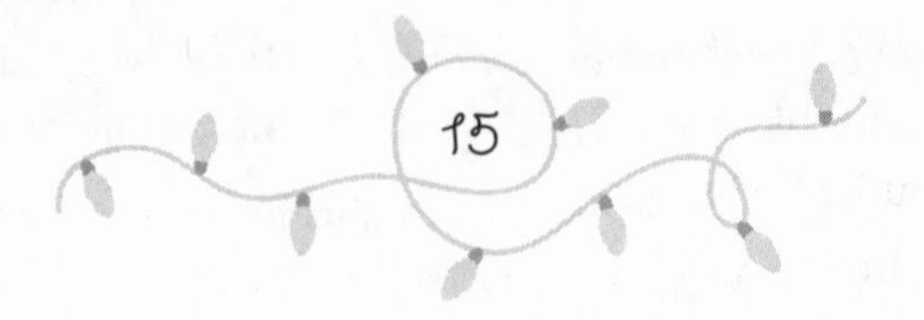

In the Mayor's Office

The next morning when Mrs. Stevens and Mike went into the barn to feed the dogs, they were happily surprised to find Emma and Yeti asleep together on the hay. Mike gave Emma a big hug that, after a moment, they both found a little embarrassing.

As Emma explained her adventure, Mrs. Stevens and Mike were both awed and angered. "Dogfights?" Mrs. Stevens exclaimed. "Norman Doyle selling dogs to dogfights?!" Mrs. Stevens immediately called Coach Cullimore for advice. He came out to the farm and had a long talk with Emma. While Emma admitted that she had stretched the truth a bit in the past, she insisted that this time her story was true.

Coach Cullimore believed her. It was a talent he had: looking into the eyes of kids and knowing if they were telling the truth or not. He told Mrs. Stevens that they should report the dogfights and Norman's involvement to the mayor. Mrs. Stevens was skeptical.

"You just haven't lived here long enough to understand how it works," Cathy told the coach. "They're brothers."

"Look, did we come through on feeding the dogs or not?"

Cathy had to admit that they had.

"Come on, let's do it!"

The coach's enthusiasm was convincing, and Cathy had no choice but to agree. Coach gave Cathy a big kiss on the forehead, making her laugh.

They took Emma into town and into the mayor's office. It was big and paneled in wood and very brown with importance. Nobel Doyle sat at his desk behind a large brass nameplate that announced that he was the mayor of Doverville, which, of course, everyone already knew. But he loved that nameplate and had it polished every day.

"And you did all that to save a dog?" Mayor Doyle said with disbelief after Emma had explained about the dogfights.

"She was Mikey's dog. And I had promised him."

"Tell the mayor about the other man you saw," the coach said to Emma, "and about the money."

CHAPTER 15

"Hello, folks!" Norman Doyle entered the room all smiles tinged with venom, holding old Scratch. "Sorry I'm late."

Late? Cathy and the coach and Emma had not even known he was invited.

"Norman!" Nobel happily greeted his brother, and then turned to Emma. "Well, who was this other man you say you saw, young lady?"

Emma felt something at the back of her neck, something cold and crawling. She turned and looked up at Norman, who was standing behind her. It had been his eyes, staring out of his malevolent face, which had bored into the back of her neck. And now they said silently: Don't talk; don't you dare talk.

"Well, who was it you saw, young lady?" the mayor asked again, impatient with this little girl.

Emma remembered her bravery of the night before, but also the danger. "It was pretty dark."

"Too dark to see their faces?"

"It was night," Emma said in a near mumble. She felt as if Norman had not just his eyes but his cold, clammy hands on the back of her neck.

"So," the mayor suggested with a hint of triumph, "you really couldn't see the men at all?"

Concerned, the coach put an encouraging hand on Emma's left shoulder; Mrs. Stevens put her hand on

Emma's right and gave it a tender squeeze. There was warmth there, warmth enough to drive away the cold and clammy. Emma looked back up at Norman. His face was no longer malevolent, just dumb and mean. "The lanterns made it pretty bright; I could see their faces just fine." Norman's face now was not just dumb but dumb*struck*. "Mr. Doyle, the dogcatcher, was the man who took the money."

There, done, Emma thought, relieved, *this should be the end of it.* But instead of the mayor immediately ordering the arrest of Norman, he sat there in disbelief.

"You say it was Norman?" *Not my baby brother,* the mayor thought. *She must be mistaken.*

But Emma confirmed it. "Yes, sir."

Mayor Doyle placed two hands on his desk and rose up from his chair to look down at the accuser of his beloved little brother. "I can assure you, young lady, that none of the scalawags you say you saw were civil servants of this town, and it certainly wasn't my brother."

"She is telling the truth, your honor." The coach came to Emma's defense.

"Well, let us be honest with one another now. We are at great odds over the issue of dogs. Why, you might even say that Mrs. Stevens and I are commanders of opposing forces. Any tactic you may use, including this farfetched accusation of my brother, is understandable. But really, Mrs. Stevens, getting a child to lie for you!"

Mrs. Stevens tried to protest, but the mayor was in a speech-making mood.

"It will surprise you, my dear Mrs. Stevens, but I am not personally *against* dogs. I am only *for* the law. I ran on a dogless platform, and dogless Doverville shall be! Unless and until the Town Council changes the law, I am duty-bound. And so is my brother, Norman."

Cathy, the coach, and Emma left the mayor's office more troubled than when they had arrived.

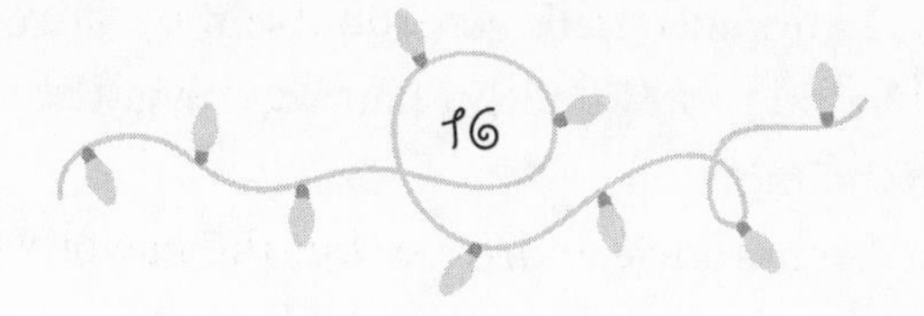

A Small Change of One Heart

Is there anything more wonderful than a Christmas tree? It is not just that it is a tree—a pretty wonderful thing in itself—it is that people have decorated it with things bright and shiny, or things, as Mrs. Stevens might say, "fraught with meaning," things that bring back memories, or things that spur on hope. To stare, not just at a Christmas tree, but into a Christmas tree, in and among the branches where a beautiful ribbon or a bright green light or a strand of tinsel or an ornament made by hand by a loved one can all say to you: there *is* hope, there *is* goodness, there *is* kindness, and there *is* joy. Is there anything more comforting than this on a cold winter's night when the spirit has been dampened?

On the way home from the mayor's office, driving

through the woods, Mrs. Stevens suddenly pulled over and stopped. "Let's go cut ourselves a Christmas tree," she said to Mike who had waited in the truck during the meeting.

"But we never get our tree until Christmas Eve," Mike said.

"I know," his mother answered, "but we *need* it now." So they marched through the woods and found just the right tree, cut it down, put it into the back of the truck, and took it home.

Emma was thrilled. It was the first Christmas tree she had had in years. As they decorated it, and moment by moment it became more than just a tree, they all began to feel better. They were still sad, and they were still worried, but hope brightened with the glow of the colorful lights.

When Mrs. Stevens went to the kitchen to make dinner, Mike asked Emma if she believed in miracles.

"No," Emma told him honestly.

"That's sad." Mike was equally honest. "Mom says that if you have faith, good things will happen. Even miracles. Getting Yeti back was a miracle."

But what was the use of that miracle? Emma wondered. *I was the one who got Yeti back. But to what good? Dogcatcher Doyle will soon take Yeti away again, won't he?* Emma wanted to be an adventure hero again. She wanted to be able to walk into the mayor's office and beat him and his dumb brother to a pulp! But she knew she couldn't do that. No matter what they had done or were going to do to the dogs, that wouldn't be right. Maybe what they needed was a real miracle to change the town of Doverville. "How do you know when something is a miracle," she wondered aloud, "or just something that would have happened anyway?"

"You just believe," Mike said. "You have faith. You know it in your heart."

Suddenly Emma clearly understood. Changes don't happen with fists; changes happen in the heart.

"Did you make a Christmas wish, Emma?" Mrs. Stevens asked when she returned.

"She wishes her dad would come and get her," Mike answered for her.

It was the wrong answer. Emma did not have to wish for her father to come. She had faith; she knew he would come. As she looked at her puppy tangled in Christmas lights, she knew the miracle she really hoped for: "I wish we could save the dogs."

That wish was on Emma's mind the next morning as they once again rehearsed "The Twelve Days of

Christmas." It was going rather smoothly now, with the kids singing in tune—thanks to Mrs. Stevens's fine piano playing—and making their moves with grace and effectiveness—thanks to Coach's game plan. Emma's part was fairly simple. During most of the song she stood at the back of the stage, then moved forward whenever it was her turn to sing, "And a partridge in a pear tree." Maybe this is why only she noticed the side door to the assembly hall opening now and then, and Principal Walsh sticking her head in ever so slightly. At first she scowled, which was normal with her, but then, could it be that Emma saw her smiling at the caroling children? Now, that *would* be a miracle.

"Okay, okay," Coach Cullimore, applauding the kids, said, "now this is the part where Santa Claus comes in. Where's Mikey?"

No, Mike was not Santa Claus. He was far too young, short, and beardless to play the role. But every Christmas program needs a Santa. Old Jake would have been perfect, but nobody, not even Emma, thought he would agree. The mayor with a fake beard might pass muster, but the jolly spirit was missing, even if anyone had wanted him. It was Mike who came up with the solution. It was daring, and it was risky—they all knew that. But it was so right. Out on the stage, to the sound of Mrs. Stevens playing "Santa Claus Is Coming to Town," came an enthusiastic Yeti in Santa hat and cloak, dragging Mike behind her on a leash.

Mrs. Walsh looked in just as Yeti sat on the stage. Emma watched as the outrage on the principal's face melted into an astonished smile. And this time, Emma knew without a doubt that a miracle was on its way.

But how? Emma kept wondering as the rehearsal ended, and as they climbed into the truck, and as they drove back to the farm. She kept thinking about it as "The Twelve Days of Christmas" kept playing in her head over and over and over, and as images of dogs, lots of dogs, kept coming to mind, four Cocker Spaniels and ten Dalmatians, six Chihuahuas and five Golden Retrievers—five Golden Retrievers? *Fiiive Goool-den Retrievers!*

"I know how we can save the dogs!" Emma blurted out, nearly causing Mrs. Stevens to swerve off the road. She quickly explained her plan, and Mrs. Stevens quickly made a U-turn and headed back to the school. Coach Cullimore needed to hear this. This was going to be wonderful!

CHAPTER 16

Coach heard it and liked it, liked it a lot. He knew, though, that nothing could be done without Mrs. Walsh giving her blessing, which he was not sure she would. But Emma was, for Emma thought she now knew something about Mrs. Walsh's heart.

The coach, Emma, and Mike met with Mrs. Walsh in her office. She was not happy about being disturbed so late in the day. They put the proposal to her, telling her they would be really careful and not wreck anything. She heard everything with a stony face.

"You are asking me to bless an outrageous idea that violates the most fundamental rules of this school, not to mention the law. I have already looked the other way to my awful shame."

The coach and Mike didn't understand, but Emma knew what she was talking about. It was, in fact, what she was counting on. Emma stood up and addressed Mrs. Walsh directly. "We really need your help. It's the only way we can save the dogs."

Mrs. Walsh stood up. "We needn't take more time on this," she said, and then she ushered the three out of her office.

Emma was confused. She was convinced that she had found something in Mrs. Walsh's heart that should have come to their aid. Maybe she was wrong; maybe that something was missing from her heart. She had to know. She walked boldly back into Mrs. Walsh's office. "You've never had a dog, have you?" she asked. Mrs. Walsh did not answer. She just kept her face like a stone and dismissed Emma with her eyes.

But as soon as Emma left, those eyes turned sad and moist. Mrs. Walsh looked at a drawer in her desk, one she rarely opened. After a moment's hesitation, she opened the drawer and took from it a photo in a tarnished silver frame. It was a photo of her, many years ago, long before her face became like a stone. She was sitting and leaning against a most magnificent Golden Retriever, a dog surely as big as she. His name had been Teddy, named for a president of the United States, and he had been killed in his prime by one of the newfangled horseless carriages. She remembered crying, crying for days, and never wanting to cry like that again. So no more dogs, no more pets, no more caring. But that darn Sheepdog in the Santa outfit! It made her smile just thinking about it. And that Emma, she was such a pest and a nuisance, but so determined, so caring for those dogs. "Oh, why not?!" Mrs. Walsh said to herself. It made her smile again to think how Emma and the others would react.

CHAPTER 16

Emma could have reacted by jumping up and down and yelling with a feeling of triumph. This is how Mike reacted, and Mrs. Stevens, and the coach, when Mrs. Walsh called and said that after serious reconsideration she had decided to give her blessing. But Emma's reaction was more quiet, more of happiness for Mrs. Walsh than a feeling a triumph for them. For Emma knew that a small change of one heart had happened. And if a small change of one heart had happened, maybe a miraculous change of many hearts would happen.

Emma knew that miracles were out of her hands. But she, along with her friends, could certainly help to prepare the town for one. And they only had six days!

The first thing to do was to gather all the kids to explain Emma's plan, and they did that at the Stevens barn. After all their time in rehearsals, the kids might have been upset at the idea of having to learn new words and new moves, but they weren't; they embraced the idea with delight. It was for the dogs! It was for Doverville.

Writing had to be done, and Emma, Mike, and Miranda took charge of that. And a whole new concept for the staging had to be worked out, and all the kids contributed to that. A set had to be built, and Coach and the handiest boys took charge of that. It was all hard work, and the kids were devoting all their spare time to it, but it was fun. It all went smoothly until they suddenly realized that while they had two of this kind, and four of that kind, and even ten of this kind, they did not have seven of any kind. And as twelve mutts were being saved for the end, they were in trouble. Then Emma thought of Old Jake and his seven Huskies.

Emma tramped through the woods out to Old Jake's place, and the dogs greeted her like an old friend. Even Old Jake was happy to see her. However, he would not agree to let her use his dogs.

"I can't risk letting them out of my sight. Not with that crazy man and the dog-haters sneaking around."

"But that's why we're doing it. To stop them," Emma pleaded.

"Not with my dogs."

Emma was disappointed, but refused to let it get everyone down. "Something will come up. Maybe some of the new dogs coming in on the train tomorrow . . ."

The train did not come in with any new dogs to fill the gap. But two days later Old Jake did. He said his seven Huskies were howling to be on Broadway!

CHAPTER 16

Everything looked set. The kids were tired, and the adults were exhausted, but they were all excited. Now there were just two more things to do. Mrs. Stevens picked up the phone and told the operator, "I would like to place a call to Lucy Stark at *LIKE* magazine." That took care of one. The other they could do at Mayor Doyle's big Christmas party, to which the whole town had been invited.

Mayor Nobel Doyle's house was a grand house. If it had been in New York City, it would not have been a grand house, or even if it had been in Pittsburgh. In those cities it would have been a rather ordinary house. But in Doverville, where most people, quite frankly, cared little about the grand, it was considered a grand house. It had been built in the Queen Anne style and had a tower at one end. It seemed royal, and anything royal was supposed to be grand.

The Doyles had always gone all out in decorating it at Christmastime, and people loved to look at it at night, sitting there in the snow, the Doyles' Christmas tree standing in its joyful glory in one of the big windows.

Emma had never been to such a party, nor to

such a house. One of the dresses Dolores had given her turned out to be perfect for the occasion. Mike had been turned into a gentleman with a suit and tie, his bright red hair slicked down and combed very neatly. He thought his mother, in a special dress she had not worn for years, was probably the most beautiful woman in the world. Coach Cullimore, who had put on his Sunday best and had driven out to the farm to pick them up, would not have disagreed.

As they entered the house brightly decorated in holly and lights, the guests thought it seemed to reflect back the warmth and joy of the season that the guests were feeling. *This was not the house of a villain in an adventure story,* Emma observed. It wasn't all dark and foreboding, as she might have expected. It made her feel good, and confident, about her plan.

Mayor Doyle addressed the guests from the middle of the staircase. "Merry Christmas, my friends, to one and all."

Then Mrs. Stevens took from Coach Cullimore a large Christmas-wrapped box that he had carried in and approached the mayor. The mayor was quite surprised to see Mrs. Stevens, even though he had invited the whole town. He was a little nervous as to what she was planning. But she came up to him smiling sweetly and said, "Mayor, I would be pleased if you would open my gift tonight."

A gift? He had not expected a gift. For a fleeting moment he thought it might be a bomb.

"Open it, please," Emma said from the crowd. "Do it for us." The crowd agreed that he should, and Mayor Doyle was never one to disagree with a crowd.

The mayor opened the lid of the box in Mrs. Stevens's hands and found that the gift was worse than a bomb. It was a puppy, the most handsome golden Labrador puppy he had ever seen. Out of the crowd welled up a collective "*Awwwww!*" that was more potent than any majority vote, and the mayor felt compelled to pick up the puppy. The puppy was warm, nicely warm, and the mayor made the effort to seem pleased. Then he noticed a giant tag on the dog. The mayor looked it over, then read it out loud, as it was addressed not just to him. "His Honor the mayor and the distinguished members of the Town Council are cordially invited to attend a holiday tribute to our town. School Assembly Hall. Six o'clock in the evening. Christmas Eve."

"To the spirit of the town and the spirit of the season," Cathy pointedly said to the mayor.

What's this all about? the mayor wondered. *What have they got planned?* Whatever it was, they had thrown down the gauntlet graciously, and he had no choice but to respond graciously. "The mayor," he addressed the crowd officially, "and the Town Council cordially accept."

The crowd seemed pleased, and that pleased the mayor. Then Cathy took back the puppy, which the mayor was happy to relinquish. "He'll be waiting Christmas morning," she said, "if you've been a good boy."

The crowd cheered and applauded, even more pleased, but this time the mayor was not pleased. It seemed that Cathy Stevens had just made a not-so-subtle step toward bringing dogs back into town.

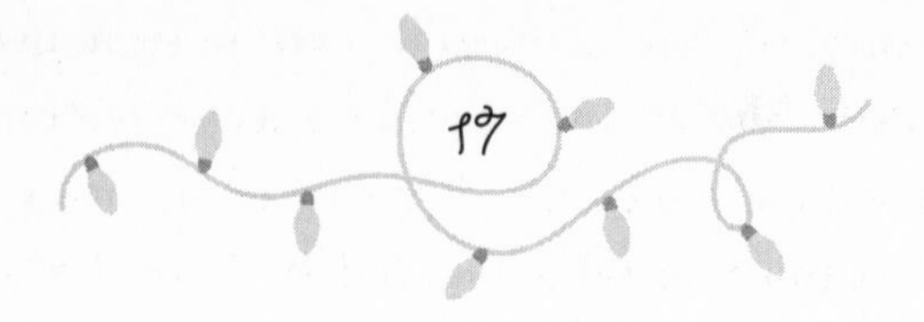

A Canine Christmas Eve

Dolores Snively woke up Christmas Eve morning a little bit sad. This had been the case for many Christmas Eve mornings, and it had always been even worse on Christmas Day mornings. For she would wake up alone, and the house would be cold, and there would be very little to look forward to. She wondered if she should even turn on the lights on the small Christmas tree she had put up in the salon. She did it for her customers; she did all her seasonal decorating for her customers. But there would be no customers today, and certainly none tomorrow, so why even turn on the lights? But she did, standing for a moment by the tree, looking at green and red and yellow lights glowing.

She marched herself into her kitchen to make a cup

of coffee, and was just taking cream out of the refrigerator when she was startled by several gentle knocks on the door. She sprung up and turned to see Emma, all bundled up, standing in her kitchen doorway.

"It's six thirty in the morning! What in the name of heaven—"

"I'm sorry it's so early, but—"

"Forget it," Dolores said, and then took a nice, deep breath. "Where's your pup? Is he all right?"

Emma nodded. "Yes, he's fine. I just need to ask you something."

"First, listen . . . I've been thinking," Dolores said, "that if you, if you wanted to come back here with me, I would be happy to have your dog and, well, forget about Norman!"

Emma gave Dolores a great big hug. It surprised Emma as much as it surprised Dolores.

Emma looked up at Dolores and smiled sweetly. "I have one more favor to ask: can you groom dogs too?"

It was the one thing in all their plans they had forgotten: the dogs needed to be dolled up! They figured it out late the night before after their last rehearsal. They were all tired and felt a little worse for the wear, but that was nothing compared to the dogs that had worked just as hard. Some had matted fur, some had fur mud-splattered, some had straw tangled in their fur, and none of their coats had the luster they deserved for being such good troupers.

"They need beauty treatments," Miranda rightly said. Beauty treatments? Well, where does one go for beauty treatments but a beauty salon? But beauty treatments for seventy-seven dogs?

"Dolores can do it." Emma was convinced.

"Not without starting very early in the morning," Mrs. Stevens added.

And that is why Emma showed up in Dolores's kitchen at six thirty in the morning, and that is why Dolores, who had woken up a little bit sad and had been expecting an empty Christmas Eve day, had, instead, a very full, very busy, and very happy day.

Of course all the kids helped, turning Dolores's Beauty Salon into a scene of canine cosmetic chaos, full of baths, bubbles, and beauty. Labradors were lathered, Dalmatians were doused, Chihuahuas were combed, Sheepdogs were shampooed, Huskies were honeyed, Boxers were bathed, Golden Retrievers were garnished, Basset Hounds were brushed, Cocker Spaniels were curled, and St. Bernards were blow-dried. Only Max the Poodle was not there, for he would not leave his doghouse. But Max was central to the plan, so plans were being made for Max.

Why are they doing this? *Max thought.* Picking up my whole doghouse—and with me in it! *It was the big man with the white beard, a very strong man, and the nice lady, not at all a weak woman, who were doing it. "Mike, don't forget the dog brushes," the lady said to the boy as she and the big man placed Max in his doghouse into the back of the truck. "You can brush Max at the school." That made Max happy. He liked being brushed, and the boy did it very well.*

Finally all seventy-seven dogs were primped, Coach Cullimore was there with the school bus, and all the dogs were excitedly loaded onto the bus by the kids for the short trip to the school. Emma was just heading toward the bus when Dolores put her arms around her and turned her back toward the house. "She's riding with me," she told Coach Cullimore. "We'll only be a minute. Come on, honey," she said to Emma, leading her back in the house.

Dolores took her right into the salon, still in a bit of a mess from the day's activity, but that did not matter. It was Emma's turn. Dolores sat her in one of the chairs, turned her toward the mirror, snatched off Emma's cloth cap, and said, "I've been waiting for this."

Emma laughed. *This*, she thought, *is going to be fun.*

It was Christmas Eve, and the school assembly hall was packed with people. There were the mayor and the Town Council, parents and teachers, Mrs. Walsh, and two people not from town: an attractive woman and a man carrying a big camera. In one corner of the hall was a beautiful Christmas tree, and its multicolored glow gave the room a cheerful air. On the stage before the curtain stood a sign on an easel that read: THE TWELVE DAYS OF CHRISTMAS—A TRIBUTE TO OUR TOWN.

Behind the curtain and backstage, the kids were hurriedly getting into costumes and hoping they remembered the newly written lyrics. The dogs were being led to their waiting places by kid stagehands in charge. And Coach and Mrs. Stevens were overseeing it all, hoping they could pull it off without a hitch.

They were running late, because Emma was not there yet. And they couldn't start without Emma.

Mayor Doyle, who did not really want to be there, stood up and announced, "Well, it seems that this tribute to our town has become a trial of our patience. I think we've done our civic duty. Merry Christmas, everyone." And with that he began to leave, the Town Council getting up to do the same.

But the attractive lady from out of town called out to stop him. "Mayor Doyle?" At first he tried to ignore her, as he knew she was not a voter, but when she gave him her name, "I'm Lucy Stark with *LIKE* magazine," he suddenly found her quite interesting.

"*LIKE* magazine! Very nice to meet you," the mayor said as he enthusiastically pumped her hand.

"Yes, we're doing a follow-up on the orphaned dogs story. Can we get a picture?"

"Of course," the mayor said smiling as the photographer snapped a picture in a flash.

"Now, was it your idea, Mayor Doyle, to have the children celebrate your most unique community with a special tribute?"

"Well, uh, actually . . ."

"It's such a fabulous idea! Another picture?"

Flash! went the photographer's bulb, bringing blinding brightness to the mayor's broad smile.

"We're going to use the follow-up as a cover story as well."

"Yes, well, it was pretty much *my* idea," the mayor fibbed.

Where was Emma? The kids were all costumed, the dogs were all in place, but where was Emma? Everyone backstage wondered and worried. Finally Emma entered through the back door, in a white Christmas dress, a candy cane vest, and large pink ribbons holding two smoothly flowing pigtails. No longer the tomboy, Emma was a beautiful young lady. Dolores came in behind her, beaming about her handiwork.

The full cast assembled, everyone made ready to start. Mrs. Stevens went into the hall to play the piano, Coach prepared himself to give all the cues, the stagehands took hold of the ropes that would open the curtains, and Emma made her way to the wings from where she would make her entrance.

On Coach's cue, Mrs. Stevens filled the room with the introduction to "The Twelve Days of Christmas."

Emma parted the curtains and walked out onto the stage. She was not nervous—she was determined.

"No one really knows for sure where the song 'The Twelve Days of Christmas' came from. Some believe it is over four hundred years old. But our program tonight is not about the twelve *days* of Christmas." Then Stephanie from the third grade came out with a small piece of cardboard that she affixed over the word *days* on the sign. On it was the word *dogs*.

"It is about the gift of friendship," Emma continued. "Friendship is what makes a town like ours so wonderful." Her puppy then came out on stage, and Emma kneeled to hold and pet it. "But some of our best friends are not welcomed here. So we thought you should get to know our friends and see why we love them so much. And, well, maybe you will learn to love them as well."

Emma went back behind the curtain, followed by the puppy. The music swelled, the curtains opened, and the audience was greeted by a beautiful, multi-level set depicting a fireplace that, oddly, had a doghouse on top of it. It was Max's doghouse, and inside was Max. Standing next to him was Miranda's six-year-old sister, Amanda (the sisters collectively known as the Andas). If Miranda was the smartest kid in school, certainly Amanda was the most adorable. On either side of the doghouse was a chorus of kids in white gowns with gold tinsel crowns. Large snowflakes hung from the rafters, and the audience sat with their mouths open in delight.

What am I doing here with all these kids? *Max thought.* What is happening? *Max looked out at all the people.* Is Mr. Whiteside out there? *he wondered.* I don't see him. Oh—they're singing. *"ON THE FIRST DAY OF CHRISTMAS, MY TRUE LOVE GAVE TO ME." The little girl started petting him. "Good boy, Max. Are you ever gonna come out of the doghouse? A POODLE IN A DOGHOUSE!"*

The audience laughed, and more than one of the women said, "Oh, how cute!" Then out of the fireplace emerged two large St. Bernards being led on leashes by boys. "ON THE SECOND DAY OF CHRISTMAS, MY TRUE LOVE GAVE TO ME," the chorus sang, "TWO ST. BERNARDS." Then Amanda sang out, "AND A POODLE IN A DOGHOUSE!"

And so it went, through "THREE COCKER SPANIELS," and "FOUR BASSETT HOUNDS," and the drawn out, and beautifully sung, FIIIIVE GOLDDEN RETRIEVERS," all illustrated by bringing onto the stage the numerically correct amount of each breed, who were led to green and red steps, and each time punctuated by Amanda's solo of "AND A POODLE IN A DOGHOUSE!" Then up the aisle, among the audience, six fine Boxers were led to the stage while the chorus sang, "SIX BOXERS BOXING!"

The audience, except possibly for Mayor Doyle, was delighted and, unfortunately, unaware that tragedy loomed. For Dogcatcher Doyle was skulking backstage looking for mischief to make. He snuck a peek of the stage just as they were singing, "SEVEN HUSKIES HOWLING!" and almost became sick to his stomach over the sight of all those illegal dogs bringing joy to people. Something had to be done. He looked around and found waiting, unattended in one corner, some dogs tied up and some in cages, numbering twelve. They were not of any matched breed but were, indeed, the climax of the show, for they were to be the TWELVE MUTTS A-MARCHING. Norman did not know this, of course, but he knew they wouldn't be there if they weren't important. So he let them go. He untied the tied ones, and uncaged the caged ones, and shooed them out of the theater to the strains of "EIGHT SHEEPDOGS SNORING!" and his own cackling laugh.

On stage there were now NINE CHIHUAHUAS

CHOMPING in the laps of nine gaily dressed kindergartners. Then the music changed to hints from the *Nutcracker*, and out of the fireplace came ten ballerinas, led by Miranda, followed by ten Dalmatians as the chorus sang, "TEN DALMATIANS DANCING."

Emma watched offstage, thrilled that it was all going well, and that the audience was responding. Maybe many small changes were happening in many large hearts right now. But as eleven Chocolate Lab puppies were being brought on stage and the kids sang, "ELEVEN LABS A-LAUGHING," in her ear came an urgent, "Emma, all the dogs for the twelfth day ran away!" At first Emma didn't believe the stagehand, but he insisted, so she went backstage to see for herself and found Norman standing there, a gleeful grin on his face and old Scratch in his arms.

"Oh, looking for the doggies?" Norman taunted just as Emma could hear, "ON THE TWELFTH DAY OF CHRISTMAS MY TRUE LOVE GAVE TO ME—" And then the music stopped, and she could hear the buzz of the audience as nothing numbering twelve happened. "On the twelfth day of Christmas," Norman sang, rather badly, "my true love gave to me—ab-so-lute-ly no doggies!"

In the assembly hall the audience was perplexed, Mrs. Walsh was consternated, and the mayor was delighted. Mrs. Stevens wondered what had happened, but figured that she had to continue, so she played the intro again, and the kids sang once more, "ON THE TWELFTH DAY . . ." But nothing more happened this time than did the last.

"What have you done with them?" Emma demanded.

Norman chuckled. "Well, I just let them out for a little walk."

There was going to be no change in this heart, Emma knew, but something had to be done. Mrs. Stevens was playing the intro once again. Emma walked right up to Norman, who hugged old Scratch closer. *Changes do not happen with fists,* Emma reminded herself, *but maybe they can be helped along now and then by a swift kick in the shin.* And so she gave Norman one, stunning him and causing him to loosen his grip on old Scratch, which she snatched away.

"ON THE TWELFTH DAY OF CHRISTMAS MY TRUE LOVE GAVE TO ME . . . ," the kids sang once again.

There was a moment of silence, a very short moment, but to Mrs. Stevens and Coach Cullimore, to Mrs. Walsh and Dolores, and especially to the kids, it seemed a very long moment indeed.

Then out of the fireplace, like the hero to the rescue

she was, ran Emma with Scratch, which she held up high for all to see. "A CAT!" Emma shouted out.

"A CAT!" the kids repeated, surprised and delighted. Mrs. Stevens finished playing with a flourish and laughed in relief, as Coach came up to her and gave her a kiss. The twinkle-eyed photographer from *LIKE* magazine snapped for posterity the picture of Emma holding up old Scratch, and the audience broke into thunderous applause—led by none other than Mayor Nobel Doyle himself!

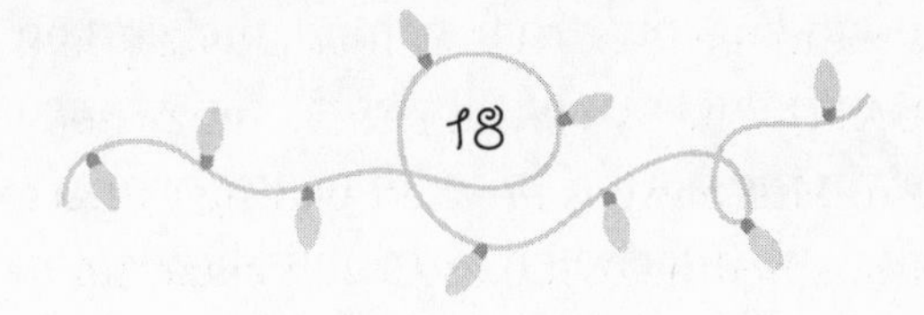

A Triple Reunion

The one person not applauding, of course, was Norman. He grabbed the ropes, closed the curtains, and ran to Emma to snatch old Scratch back. "Gimme my cat! Gimme *my* cat!" Unfortunately, this placed him right in the middle of many dogs, some of which had a very good memory of exactly who Norman was.

The audience was still on its feet, many were still applauding, and *all* were excitedly chatting about what a great show they had just seen, when they suddenly heard a great disturbance from behind the curtain. There was growling and barking and squealing (this from Norman), and the curtain was being kicked into a great agitation. Suddenly old Scratch came bounding out from behind the curtain and jumped into the arms of the sheriff for protection.

"What in the world?" more than one person asked.

The answer came when Mike and Miranda opened the curtains to reveal Norman on the floor, desperately struggling under a pile of dogs, none of which were actually hurting him, some of which were just licking him—an act that Norman did not appreciate at all. Kids ran in and grabbed the dogs, taking them away, leaving Norman defeated on the floor. Next to him, obviously having fallen from his pocket during the struggle, and in plain sight to everyone—including the mayor—was a large wad of money.

The mayor was stunned. So it was true! His brother! A dogfight profiteer! Nobel Doyle marched onto the stage, took the wad of money, and shook it in Norman's face. "Dogfights, Norman?" Nobel said in utter disappointment. Then with anger he ripped from Norman's overalls the patch that read: DOG-CATCHER OF DOVERVILLE leaving behind the old one which read: GARBAGE COLLECTOR. "And that cat goes back to sanitation with you!" With that, the mayor left the stage to rejoin the warmth of the cheering crowd.

Emma could not have been more pleased. Well,

no, that is not true. Something could have pleased her even more. And in thinking about her father, she saw what she assumed was a momentary illusion, maybe a wish-induced mirage. But the image hung on, stayed there in the back of the hall, standing in the colors of the Christmas tree, clapping and smiling. *Oh my goodness!* Emma realized. *It's not an illusion; it's not an illusion at all!* She ran off the stage, up the aisle, and into the arms of her father. They hugged; they hugged so tightly they both had to catch their breath when they broke.

"You came!" Emma said.

"Of course I came. You were wonderful."

"But Aunt Dolores said, I mean, I thought—you really came."

"Nothing's more important than a promise, Em."

Emma grabbed her father again and hugged him tightly. "I love you, Dad."

"I love you too, Emma."

It was all a bit confusing for Max—the applauding, the cheering, the dogs playing with that funny-looking human. But wasn't it time to go? He could use a little rest. Actually he would like to have joined the others. It looked like they

were having fun, but how could he have fun without Mr. Whiteside?

"Max!" Why he could almost hear Mr. Whiteside calling him. "Max!"

Wouldn't it be wonderful if—wait! Max looked down from the doghouse on top of the fireplace and looked into the eyes of Mr. Whiteside. But was it really Mr. Whiteside? He seemed to have four legs now, two of them wooden, and one of his old legs was covered in white. "Don't you recognize me, Max?" Yes, of course, it was Mr. Whiteside! Max jumped out of the doghouse onto the green and red steps and ran to Mr. Whiteside, wanting to jump up on him. "Whoa, careful, boy. I'm a bit unsteady on my feet. Here, let me sit." Mr. Whiteside sat on one of the steps, then took Max's head in his hands and gave him a big kiss. "Oh, it's so good to see you, Max. I wasn't sure I was going to make it. It's hard to ride the rails in a cast. Yes, look, I have a broken leg. Isn't it wonderful?! You see, I was yelling at those careless men taking my furniture away when I leaned a bit too far out of the window. Thank goodness they had piled all the mattresses on the sidewalk. Fell right on top of them. Of course, then I bounced off of them onto the sidewalk, and that's when I broke my leg. But a blessing in disguise, Max, a blessing in disguise, for while I was in the hospital, Max, the pain meant nothing, but the missing of you was unbearable. So I decided not to bear it, no matter what! And here I am! I don't know what we're going to do, Max. Maybe when my leg gets better, we can ride the rails out West. Who knows? But whatever may come, at least we'll be together."

Max was happy. And he didn't care if he ever saw another doghouse in his life.

On the other side of the Christmas tree was Dolores, who had been waiting for Emma. She had not seen Douglas O'Connor enter, and saw him only when Emma ran into his arms. She felt a little awkward, and thought she should leave, but Douglas saw her and went over to her, holding out his hand. "Thank you," Douglas said. Dolores wasn't sure whether she should take his hand or not. "I'm not the man you knew," Douglas continued, "and I apologize for the man I was. Many things have happened to me in the years since we knew each other. Some good—Emma's mother—a lot bad. But I'm here today to tell you that I'm determined to work hard to make nothing but good things for my daughter and me from now on."

"Yeah," Dolores said, still skeptical. "Work hard at what?"

Douglas smiled. "You are looking at the brand

new Northeastern United States sales representative for Jell-O."

"Jell-O?"

"Hey, it's light and sweet. And if this country ever needed anything light and sweet . . ."

"Jell-O?"

"They just introduced a new flavor—lime!"

"Jell-O?"

"They're going to sponsor the Jack Benny radio show!"

"Jell-O?"

"Okay, it's commission only, but I know I can do it. I'll travel to every city and town and little country store in the Northeast and become the top salesman, I swear. And I can base right here in Doverville, because, you know, I always loved this place. But, because I'm going to be traveling most the time, I need someone to help take care of Emma, and so, I thought . . ."

Dolores finally took Douglas's hand and shook it warmly. "I *love* Jell-O!" she said most emphatically.

Epilogue

Three weeks later there was a historic picture on the cover of the *Doverville Trumpet.* It showed the leading citizens of Doverville gathered at the Stevens farm around a large sign that read: THE CITY OF DOVERVILLE & THE STEVENS FAMILY DOG ORPHANAGE. The orphanage was now official, funded by the city, as unanimously approved by the Town Council, and by the flood of donations in pennies, nickels, dimes, and the occasional dollar bill that had come in ever since the second *LIKE* magazine article had appeared.

In the picture you could plainly see the mayor on one side of the sign, and Emma, who had just unveiled the sign at the mayor's invitation, on the other side. You could also see many happy dogs and lots of cheerful children, and Mrs. Walsh and Mable and Old Jake, but not Norman, who was busy collecting garbage, nor bug-face Melvin, who was busy helping him.

To one side you could see Mike kneeling by and hugging Yeti, and behind them you could see Mrs. Stevens and Coach, the only ones not looking into the camera, for they were looking at each other. And on the other side you could see Douglas O'Connor with Emma's puppy on a leash, standing next to Dolores. And if you looked very close, you could see her hand comfortably placed in his.

And you could see Max. Yes, Max, sitting proudly by Mr. Whiteside, now out of his cast. They did not decide to ride the rails to go out West, for Mr. Whiteside could tell that Max did not want to leave all his new friends, especially now that he could run around with them and play. And as no one in Doverville wanted to lose Max, or the man who showed him such great love and devotion, Mrs. Stevens offered Mr. Whiteside the position of senior dog-keeper of the dog orphanage, and Mr. Whiteside was pleased to accept.

After the picture had been taken, Emma returned to her father and Dolores and her puppy.

"Does he have a name?" her dad asked as she took the pup into her arms.

Emma thought for a moment. Then she said, "His name is Miracle."

About the Author

Steven Paul Leiva is a writer, director, and producer. He directed and co-wrote the ADA Award–nominated *Bob Bergen in Not Just Another Pretty Voice.* In film, Leiva is best known for producing the animation in *Space Jam.* Leiva also provided the voice of "Scott" in the multi-award-winning animated short *The Indescribable Nth,* which was short-listed for the Academy Award and can be viewed on Atomfilms.com. He is the doting father of two daughters and makes his home with wife, Amanda, in California.